PE

RETURN TO BHANUPUR

Giles Tillotson is well known as a writer and lecturer on Indian history and architecture. He taught at the University of London from 1990 to 2004, since when he has been living in Gurgaon, near Delhi. His earlier books include *Mughal India*, *Jaipur Nama* and *Taj Mahal*, all published by Penguin. This is his first work of fiction.

Return to
BHANUPUR
a novel

GILES TILLOTSON

PENGUIN BOOKS

An imprint of Penguin Random House

PENGUIN BOOKS

USA | Canada | UK | Ireland | Australia
New Zealand | India | South Africa | China

Penguin Books is part of the Penguin Random House group of companies
whose addresses can be found at global.penguinrandomhouse.com

Published by Penguin Random House India Pvt. Ltd
4th Floor, Capital Tower 1, MG Road,
Gurugram 122 002, Haryana, India

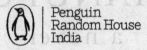

Penguin
Random House
India

First published by Penguin Books India 2012

10 9 8 7 6 5 4 3 2

ISBN 9780143414285

Typeset in Goudy Old Style by Eleven Arts, Delhi
Printed at Repro India Limited

Contents

Contents

Foreword

This is a work of fiction. Although it draws on some suggestive historical incidents, all the characters along with their thoughts and conversations are imaginary. The narrative does not present a portrait of any actual person, living or dead. My aim is to tell a story while capturing something of the spirit of an Indian court at the turn of the last century.

Despite this disclaimer, I have some anxiety that a few readers might consider my depiction of the maharaja inadequately respectful. To them I would point out that my fictional character is a more dedicated and complex individual than posterity believes many real-life maharajas to have been. Indeed, it is likely that more readers will regard my portrayal as too sympathetic. Maharajas have

not always had a good press in modern times. In the
popular mind, the stock caricature maharaja was servile
towards the British, neglectful of his duties, and given
to self-indulgence and vice. I consider this conventional
view to be both partial and severe, and I have attempted
in this novel to depict some of the challenges that
confronted such rulers and their aides and employees.
The story is offered as a tribute to those individuals
who devoted their energy and talents to India's former
princely states.

Prologue

Prologue

On the September morning when Maharaja Sir Amar Singh II died in his sleep, a sigh of relief was heard to issue from the British Residency. The Resident received the news in a brief handwritten note delivered to his desk along with his customary pre-lunch glass of gin and bitters. Having absorbed its content, he took a moment to notice the meticulous hand of the Maharaja's prime minister, still unhurried and formal even when imparting such an important message, and then grunted his approval.

'Excellent. Perhaps there is a divine providence after all.'

Reginald Slater rang for his private secretary, and when the young man presented himself in a posture of something like attention on the far side of his desk, handed him the note with the comment, 'Some good news, at last.'

The pale round face that looked up from the paper registered an evident uncertainty about how best to respond.

'Really, sir? I know he's generally thought a pretty obstinate sort of fellow. *Was* thought, I should say. But one has to admit he was magnificently regal. Bhanupur will be a poorer place without him.'

'Sometimes I wonder at reports of your intelligence, Simpson. You're alleged to have a first from Oxford, for Christ's sake! . . . Regal? I admit nothing of the sort. Our great, now late, Maharaja was nothing but a buffoon and an obstacle to any hope of progress. Having him out of the way—and with his successor a minor for the best part of the next ten years—gives us a chance to get our hands in and have a thorough clean-up.' But his expression of determination folded as he added distractedly, 'Mind you, it will be a Herculean task. Cleaning the Augean stables will have nothing on this.'

If the Resident had troubled to examine his private secretary's expression at this moment he might have noticed that he was still struggling with regret.

'Is it known what he died of, sir? The prime minister's note doesn't say.'

'Sexual exhaustion, I shouldn't wonder. Too many evenings spent in his private brothel up in Vijaygarh Fort. Come to think of it, we'd do well to start our clean-up exercise there, by turfing out his stable of painted ladies.'

'But where will they go?' The hint of concern in the young man's voice was met by a bewildered stare.

'What the deuce does it matter where they go? Having them where they are is a disgrace to the state, as my predecessors have been telling the Maharaja for the last forty years.'

Feeling snubbed, the secretary moved the conversation to a topic on which he knew he commanded his superior's confidence. 'I suppose, at least, this will be an opportunity to sort out the matter of the state revenue, sir.'

'It will indeed, Simpson. It will indeed. The whole treasury has got into a frightful mess through the interventions of Madam Nargis, or whatever she calls herself. Ghastly female.' Slater sipped his gin, wiped his moustache with his forefinger, and added ruminatively, 'By the way, touching on the revenue, what do you make of Pandit Achal?'

'The new member of the Maharaja's privy council, sir? From the few dealings I've had with him so far, he seems to me very able indeed. Sound judgement and an open and straightforward manner. Why do you ask?'

'Because I think he's one that we might draft into the regency government that we'll have to set up. Your feelings confirm my own. I think he'll make an excellent minister of finance.'

'Isn't it a little early to be thinking of all that, sir? I mean, surely there will be a period of mourning before we can do anything officially?'

'Listen, Simpson. For your own benefit, I advise you to listen carefully. One day you might find yourself in a position like mine, as Resident in a Princely State. That is assuming that you don't make a complete balls-up of your part of the job that now lies ahead of us. And if you ever are so fortunate, remember this. There is nothing better that can befall a Resident than to have his Maharaja die on him. Especially if the heir is a minor. You spend most of a normal term of office hanging about gaudy functions, giving advice that no one pays any attention to and writing reports for the Viceroy's council that nobody reads. You get a decent house, of course, and a few other perks that make life tolerable. But from a professional point of view, it's nothing but frustration. A regency government is your only chance for some real work, a chance to make a mark on the place. If that chance comes your way, you have to move decisively in the time available. You can't dilly-dally because of sensitivities at court.'

'Thank you for your insight, sir, I'll certainly bear it in mind. If, as you say, I should ever be so fortunate. But tell me, sir . . .' Simpson hesitated, wondering whether it was prudent to air the thought that had come to his mind; but seeing the Resident's quizzical eyebrows, realized that he had committed himself to finishing. 'When you speak of making a mark, I presume you mean for the benefit of the ordinary populace, the state's subjects.'

'Naturally. Who else would it be for?'

'Well, sir,' Simpson pursued cautiously, a little anxious now but still eager to know the Resident's mind, 'you may think me cynical but when you said that a regency is professionally fulfilling, it occurred to me that it might also have its rewards from . . . um . . . a career point of view as well.'

Slater eyed his secretary narrowly. He was sometimes unsure whether Simpson was being uppity or artless. He certainly never thought of him as cynical.

'Performing a difficult task well never hurt anyone's prospects, young man. It gets one noticed. But since you are so bold as to ask whether I see any personal advantage in this situation, I don't mind telling you frankly that I do. For one thing, the Hyderabad post should fall vacant in three years. My wife's uncle, Sir John Biddulph, you know, led the regency government in Gwalior back in the nineties and left with a knighthood.'

'Ah, . . . *Sir* Reginald?'

'Sound incredible to you, Simpson?'

'Not at all, sir. Devoutly to be wished for.'

'It will take more than wishing. It will take a great deal of hard graft to get the job done thoroughly. And we must get on with it without delay. You could make a start, Simpson, by drawing up a list of all those responsible citizens, including Pandit Achal, who you think we might call on for posts in the governing council. Men we can depend on to see things our way.'

'Certainly, I'll see to it immediately. Oh, . . . will the council include the Yuvraj? I should say the new Maharaja.'

'Why?'

'Because if he is to be in it, then it would be wise, might it not, to include someone who is close to him personally, whose judgement he trusts. To help guide his decisions.'

'No, I meant, why should the council include the new Maharaja?'

'Well, that would be normal, sir, wouldn't it?'

'Certainly not. He's a child of ten. No question of including him.'

'But it could be awkward, couldn't it? I mean, if he's around but not in the council, it might create resentment, even a possible rival power base.'

'But he won't be around, Simpson. I repeat, he's a child of ten. The first thing we will do is pack him off to boarding school. Mayo College, probably. That should be enough to anticipate any interference of the sort you seem to fear. Now off you go and bring me that list. We can discuss it after lunch.'

The Resident watched his secretary withdraw, and was dismayed to see him pause at the door and turn wearing a contemplative expression.

'I wonder how history will judge him.'

'Judge who?'

'The Maharaja. I mean, what will his legacy be?'

'Maharajas don't leave legacies except to their bastard offspring. All eyes now will be on the future, which is where yours should be, Simpson.'

'But he did complete the city's museum, which is still very popular . . . and his visit to London for the coronation. Many people in Bhanupur regard those as great achievements.'

'More fool them. Those were the only times he did what he was told. Something you should learn to do.' Slater glared at his secretary, forcing him to nod and finally retreat.

Picking up the remains of his gin, the Resident carried it out through the veranda onto the grass terrace at the back of the Residency. He paced its length slowly, always looking down, observing his shoes sink into the spongy turf. At the far end he paused, raised his glass to his lips and gazed out over the garden below. Everything in it looked fresher than it had just the day before. He felt a surge of enthusiasm for his position. Friends in the political service had commiserated with him on his appointment to Bhanupur a year ago, warning him, with barely concealed pleasure, that Amar Singh was the most conservative and debauched of maharajas. What would they say now he was dead?

He raised his glass again, in a toast to the flowerbeds. 'What a blessing!' he said aloud.

1887

In the early morning light, the shadows of trees lay long across the lawns. Colour had yet to reach the canna lilies, standing four-feet tall in the beds that fringed the garden, and the terracotta planters that lined the axial drive were dull and cool. In the centre of it all, the new building glistened where its eaves and parapets caught the first rays of the sun, but the intricate stonework of its arches, rising tier upon tier, still hid in a haze. Quartzite, sandstone and marble, piled high through five receding levels, defined no more than an airy ziggurat or pyramid of cages. At the highest points, the domes—designed to stand against the blue sky of noon—were slowly coming into bud.

Already on the grass before the building, a handful of workmen began the preparations for the ceremony scheduled for the following day, unrolling the awning, a thick patchwork of coloured cotton that they would raise on poles to form a covered gallery. Some called out instructions while others hammered at tent pegs or

13

swept again the broad verandas; but the sounds of their labour did not carry, dying upon the air like the cawing of the crows.

It was now eleven years since the foundation stone had been laid. Eleven years of sometimes frantic work had disturbed the peace of the Ratan Niwas Gardens, keeping the public out and provoking the ire of the gardeners, dismayed at the ruts caused by the ceaseless trundle of carriages laden with building material. Now that the construction was complete and the turf restored, the mayhem was forgiven and the building could no longer be thought an intrusion. Indeed its position made it seem inevitable, the always intended centrepiece of its setting.

The colonnades that enclosed its front courtyards marched forward, turned smartly and came together in an elaborate portico, forming a peak that pointed, across the distance of a few hundred yards, to the central gate of the old walled city. There, the heavy spiked wooden doors stood open, and past them rolled bullock carts and handcarts, each heaped high with produce, draining in from the broad road that ran the full length of the city's wall. The scene had been repeated daily for a century and a half. But the road was even older, for the city had been erected along its northern side, so as to draw its traffic in—like this—towards its markets. Beyond, to the south, there was once only emptiness and sand. Then the wasteland was transformed into a garden, from whose centre now the new building seemed to address the city directly, challenging the embattled life long held behind its pink crenellations, offering the promise of a new era, to be enjoyed in green spaces, among the lilies.

✥

'Have you written my speech for tomorrow morning, Panditji?'

The two men sat on opposing sofas in one corner of the cavernous Dilkushal Mahal, the largest and grandest of the reception rooms of the City Palace. But for the gilding and painting covering every inch of wall and ceiling, the room resembled nothing so much as a barn, and though the Maharaja and his prime minister were both men of generous proportions they made so little impact on its space that they might easily have been overlooked by anyone happening to pass through. It was not a place where they usually met to confer in private, but this morning the prime minister, seeking out his employer, had caught up with him here, and was directed to sit.

'I have the draft with me, Sarkar.'

As the Maharaja took the proffered sheet of paper, he noticed that Babu Chatterjee was sweating, though it was still only February. Glistening lines marked his ample cheeks and neck, and dark patches stained the edges of the cloth-bound portfolio from which the draft of the speech had just been extracted by a clammy hand. However did he manage in his native Calcutta, the Maharaja wondered. He glanced at the half-dozen neatly handwritten lines on the paper, and smiled his approval.

'It is commendably short. Brevity has always been one of your virtues, Panditji. For a former schoolmaster you are remarkably free of the vice of prolixity.'

'Your Highness is most generous. I have striven to keep it short—and I could get it still shorter if permitted more time to work on it—partly because I believe that there is little on this occasion that Your Highness needs to say, but largely because I anticipate rather longer offerings from the other speakers.'

'The length is perfect,' the Maharaja reassured his most assiduous courtier. He scratched at his full beard and tugged at the edge of his velvet gown to loosen its hold. 'But I notice it is in English. Are all the speeches to be in English?'

'Yes, Sarkar, that is the agreed plan.'

'Please tell me why.' His tone was despondent.

'What language would Your Highness deem more suitable for the proceedings? Sanskrit, perhaps?' The minister at once regretted this sally.

'I see you mean to trifle with me, Chatterjee Sahib,' the Maharaja objected, though failing to catch his minister's averted eye. 'I was thinking of Urdu, our language of official business. It is a state occasion, after all. But since you suggest it, yes, I think Sanskrit would be eminently appropriate. The museum that we are to open is intended, at least in part, as a display of our own state heritage, is it not? To raise a little pride in our cultural achievements in the minds of our noble citizens. Or is it meant solely for the entertainment of foreign tourists?'

'Your government certainly hopes that visitors to the state will be among those who will learn to appreciate and respect the achievements you mention, Sarkar, and that is indeed part of the museum's purpose. But there were other reasons for choosing English over Urdu or indeed Sanskrit for the opening speeches.'

'And what were they? You still haven't told me.'

'Our principal guest as you know is to be the Chief Commissioner for Rajputana, Colonel Sir Edward Grayson. I am assured, officially, that a fluency in Urdu is a requirement for anyone holding his post, but I am also assured, privately, that Sir Edward's command of the language is—how can I put it?—not so secure as to avert all possibility of embarrassment. Then there is the consideration that British ladies will also be gracing the occasion with their presence. And finally, Dr Constable has told me that if all the speeches are delivered in English he can undertake to have the full texts published in the next edition of the *Journal of Indian Art*. That, I believe, would be a great advantage to us, Your Highness.'

'Why? What is the *Journal of Indian Art*?'

'It is a new periodical, published in London. It is edited by Mr Longfellow. You may remember him,

Sarkar. He was the gentleman who came here from
Lahore back in '83, when we held our art exhibition,
to serve as the external member of the board of jurors.
Awarded all the prizes to Punjabis.'

'All the prizes, prime minister? I seem to recall the
excellent Abdul Karim getting a medal for his brassware.
I was pleased, given the work he has done for us in
the palace.'

'I was thinking particularly of the prize for damascening
on armour, Your Highness. It was awarded to a man from
Sialkot. The choice surprised me because Dr Constable,
who is an authority on the art, tells me that nothing
surpasses the work that is done here in Bhanupur.'

'The Doctor Sahib is no doubt correct. He is, as you
say, an authority on the subject. But you exaggerate in
saying all the prizes. You also digress. You haven't told me
how it is to our benefit to have the speeches published
in this journal.'

'It was Dr Constable's own suggestion, Sarkar. To
publicize the opening of the museum. It is hardly
likely to be reported in the London daily press, but
at least by this means people in Britain who are
interested in such matters will come to hear of it. Dr
Constable is of the view that the museum merits an
international reputation.'

The Maharaja shook with laughter and Chatterjee
looked put out.

'Your Highness thinks not?'

'On the contrary, I hope he's right. I was merely thinking . . . is there no limit to what the energetic doctor will do for us? He's supposed to be the Residency Surgeon, you know. I don't believe his actual brief extends much beyond giving the Resident the occasional glass of seltzer water. But here he goes charging all over the state setting up dispensaries, and in his spare time he runs his own observatory and has filled a museum . . . which he now seeks to publicize, for the greater glory of Bhanupur!'

Chatterjee's face betrayed his concern. He knew that Constable's activities were not always a safe subject. 'I do believe he gives us excellent service, Your Highness,' he began cautiously, 'and that his intentions are always sincere. Though I do also understand that Your Highness sometimes finds his enthusiasm a little trying on the patience.'

'Trying? I should say! The man's a machine. You know, I pity poor Mrs Constable. Do you suppose he regales her over dinner with his barometer readings and rainfall statistics?'

By now Chatterjee was looking shocked. 'I have no insight into his domestic arrangements, Sarkar. I am of the view that we should welcome his projects, so far as they help to advance health and learning amongst Your Highness's subjects. My only reservation is, well, a somewhat delicate, perhaps even a political matter.' He paused.

'Well, prime minister?'

'Dr Constable is a member of the Indian Medical Service. But while he is on secondment in Bhanupur, he is effectively an employee of our state. I consider it incumbent on Your Highness's government to keep this always in mind, and not allow him to run away with the credit for everything that we encourage or permit him to achieve for us. The initiative for what he does lies with the Bhanupur government, which ultimately means with yourself, Sarkar.'

'Well said! You have my full agreement. And in this connection, I especially approve what you have said about him in my speech. Where is it, now?' The Maharaja glanced over the sheet still grasped in his hand. 'Here, where you say, "The statement read by Surgeon-Major Constable will give you an idea of what has been, and what is intended to be done to make the Jubilee Hall an object of attraction." Brilliantly put, if I may say so. "Read by" hints without explicitly saying that his speech was written for him, and this next phrase, in the passive—by *not* saying done or intended *by him*—implies that he is the instrument of the government's wishes. Capital! Nothing that he can actually take exception to. But it will leave the audience in no doubt about who is in charge. I commend your subtlety, Chatterjee. More than that, I congratulate myself for recognizing that you would make a better politician than you ever were a schoolmaster.'

'I strive to serve, Sarkar. I am all gratitude for the confidence you place in me.' Privately the minister thought: 'Full marks, Maharaja. For all your jibes against schoolmasters and men of learning, you have a swift understanding. Nothing in a text escapes you.' He began to fidget with his sweat-stained portfolio, unsure whether the Maharaja's silence signalled the end of the interview. He stood, tucked the portfolio under his arm and joined his hands.

'One last thing, Panditji, before you go. Which of us will actually deliver my speech tomorrow?'

'I had thought, Your Highness, since it is short and cannot tire you to read, that you yourself might . . .'

'No,' the Maharaja interrupted, handing back the paper without getting up. 'It would be better if you read it for me. It would send the wrong signal for me to read a speech in English, in front of British people.'

'Signal, Sarkar? What signal would it send?'

'The British are our excellent allies. But it doesn't do to get too close to them. If I start addressing them in their own language they might start to think me approachable.'

❀

'How's your drink doing, Constable? There's time for another, I think.'

The host flapped a hand towards the bearer standing by the veranda door, dressed in a scarlet tunic. As the man approached, the hand—broad and backed with coils of wiry white hair—hung poised in the air and then pointed towards the glass still held by the doctor, while a mellow voice urged, 'Whisky-soda *lao*.'

Constable wearily raised his glass to the tray presented at his elbow and, as the bearer withdrew, let his hand flop onto the arm of the cane chair. He was not really tired, merely relaxed, as he always felt in his friend's bungalow. He looked around the familiar veranda, noticing the midges that were already collecting around the lantern hanging on the wall. He liked this time of day when the darkness fell swiftly like a curtain, to signal the end of another day's work. He especially liked spending it with Colonel Talbot, the only person with whom he could discuss work entirely freely, confident of not being a bore. He now studied Talbot's figure seated opposite him, back to the garden, the face half concealed by darkness but lit by sparkling eyes and the large blond walrus moustache, luminous and twitching.

'Dare I ask,' Talbot said gently, 'what you made of this morning's proceedings?'

'Huh!' An exhalation and a wry smile were at first Constable's only response, but then he collected himself. 'I thought the Jubilee Hall was looking splendid. Really splendid. It was a joy to see it animated by a crowd for the first time, after so many months—*years*—of work. And with all the workmen's dust cleared away, one could appreciate the stonework properly. I know there's still more to do.

Until we get the murals finished the building won't be fully complete, and of course there's much to be done on labelling the collections, but one has a sense now of how it will be.'

'And the speeches? How did they strike you?' Talbot's steady gaze revealed a wish to probe and his awareness that his companion had avoided the question intended.

But Constable still resisted. 'I thought Grayson's was long and predictable,' he said. 'It amazes me how little these fellows in the Political Service really know about what goes on in the Princely States. Lots of bland reminders of the benefits flowing to Bhanupur from its treaty with the Crown, but hardly a word of recognition that the benefits flow equally the other way. No doubt we'll hear much more in the same vein this evening at the banquet. What time is it, by the way?'

'It's only six-thirty. We're not due there till eight. And it's at the Khasa Kothi, so you can go home and change on the way. Ample time for you to enjoy your drink,' Talbot added on seeing the bearer reappear in the doorway and approach to place a tumbler on the glass-topped table between them. Receiving a silent half-shake of the head in response to his enquiring glance at his employer, the servant again withdrew into the house. 'And time for you to answer my question,' Talbot pursued. 'I am curious to hear your reaction to the speech by the Maharaja.'

'*Was* it by the Maharaja? I rather fancy it was written by the man who read it.'

'Well . . . your reaction to Chatterjee's speech, then.'

'He was generous enough to *you*. That at least was gratifying. "Couldn't have been done without the kind and timely help of Colonel Talbot", or some such phrase, wasn't it?'

'*Too* generous, in fact.' Talbot's tone was mollifying. 'As you know, I did little more than work out the stresses of the ironwork, and even that only on paper. Ibrahim Hussain actually carried it out, and supervised all the stonework. I myself thought . . . given that you selected all the exhibits and planned the museum display, that they might have acknowledged as much.'

'Well it's kind of you to say so, Talbot. Much appreciated. An acknowledgement from you is reward enough.' Constable sipped his whisky gratefully, as if it were part of the compliment. 'In fact, it will have to suffice,' he continued. 'I don't suppose that the Maharaja or the prime minister really can say much more than they did. Not publicly at least. In the eyes of the people they have to keep the credit to themselves. I do understand that, believe me. Even so, I thought the wording was pretty devious. "The statement *read by* Surgeon-Major Constable", as though Chatterjee had written *my* speech as well!'

'I confess that possible interpretation did occur to me at the time,' Talbot conceded. 'Chatterjee can certainly be devious, as you say. When he feels he needs to be. But he's not generally vindictive. He has a good heart.'

'Try telling that to the Manosa clan!' Constable replied derisively. Talbot's puzzled squint forced him to explain. 'You know he's fixed it so that Sajjan Singh of Manosa is to be appointed Chief of Police in Panchwati? An impossible task! Chatterjee's just setting him up to fail, waiting for a moment when he can point out his inadequacies to the Maharaja.'

'Well he may have misjudged his man if that's his game,' Talbot said judiciously. 'It's by no means a foregone conclusion that Sajjan Singh will fail.'

'In Panchwati? You'd have to be King Solomon to keep order there! What's he got against the Manosas anyway? I simply don't understand it.'

Talbot was cautious. He disliked discussing men's weaknesses, even with his friend. He ventured softly, as a suggestion ready to be dismissed, 'I imagine there may be a little envy of the influence the family exerted over late His Highness.'

'But Ratan Singhji died—what—seven years ago!' Constable protested. 'No, I'm sorry, my dear fellow, but if that truly is his reasoning then the man is indeed vindictive. You always think the best of people. It's in your nature. But our friend Chatterjee is a typical wily Bengali, and nothing else.' He took a defiant swig of whisky and replaced the tumbler heavily on the table, like a gavel.

Talbot said nothing but looked uncomfortable, and waved a hairy hand to waft the aspersion away. Constable shifted in his chair, showing that he was chastened. He stared out at the night beyond the dimly lit veranda, as if watching his irritation depart. But he was not yet ready to drop the topic. He continued more quietly, 'How does he come to be here, by the way, do you know? In Bhanupur, I mean. You must have been here already, before he arrived.'

'Good heavens, yes! Mrs Talbot and I will have been here twenty years come April. Chatterjee was brought here from Calcutta by Maharaja Ratan Singh, I'd say about ten years ago. He taught English at the Maharaja's College to begin with. He only became prime minister at the start of the present reign. About the time you got here yourself.'

Constable looked thoughtful. 'Do you know what his secret passion is?' he asked; but seeing Talbot frown and clutch the end of his moustache, he quickly added, 'No, it's nothing of that sort. He collects arms and armour.'

'Good heavens!' Talbot said again. 'You mean actual weapons?'

'No, no. I don't think he's preparing for war. No, I mean the ornamental work. Like the things produced by the School of Art. Inlaid with gold and silver. Even so, doesn't quite fit with the schoolmaster image, does it?'

'How do you know this, Constable?'

'It came to light at the time of the Exhibition, back in '83. Do you remember we invited Longfellow over from Lahore to be one of the judges? And he awarded the gold prize in metal inlay work to some fellow from Sialkot. Fateh Din, I think his name was. Well, our friend Chatterjee was livid. Came and harangued me about it. Didn't I think that all the best work of this kind was made in Bhanupur, he said. Privately, I agreed with him that Longfellow had got it wrong, but you can't very well ask a chap to be an independent judge and then question his verdict. Like challenging the umpire. I had no idea why Chatterjee was so upset. Lots of the other prizes went to craftsmen from outside Bhanupur. I happened to mention it a day or two later to our chief clerk at the museum, Kashinath. And he told me that Chatterjee collects the stuff. Secretly. He daren't go into the market for it himself, because he doesn't trust the traders who might raise their prices if they knew he was interested. So Kashinath buys it for him, on commission. Apparently he has a number of first-rate pieces.'

'Well I never!' Talbot was evidently amused, but also perplexed. 'How do you explain it?' he asked. 'If you told me he collects manuscripts of the Gita Govinda, I wouldn't be at all surprised. But what possible attraction can ornamental armour hold for a man of his tastes?'

'Part of the Rajput mystique, I imagine,' Constable suggested. 'Under their bookish veneer these Bengali types often hide a deep regard for the martial Rajputs they work for, you know. They affect to despise them, of course. But deep down there's a bit of the soldier in every man. Curious way to express it, though, don't you think?'

'It rather increases my regard for him,' Talbot said indulgently. 'Do you suppose the Maharaja knows? Or does Chatterjee keep it a secret from him as well?'

'I've really no idea, Talbot. But to be honest, I have pretty little insight into the relations between those two. When you meet them together, each always seems to know exactly what's in the other's mind, as if they've been able to rehearse every possible situation in advance. Yet on the surface they seem so different from each other. Chatterjee's always the intellectual. A schoolmaster, you say. While the Maharaja . . . well, he doesn't exactly have a reputation as a man of learning, does he?'

'Rather the reverse,' Talbot conceded sadly. 'I remember when he was a child, before the late Maharaja adopted him as his heir. The Maharaja told the boy's natural father to send him to the Rajput School in the city to get some education. But it didn't take. He ran away and joined some wrestling academy. Even now he can be fairly sarcastic about academic pursuits. But the funny thing is he supports all the schools set up by his predecessor. For all the bluster, he has a sneaking regard for the life of the mind. I know for a fact that he has a high opinion of you, Constable.' As his companion snorted in objection, Talbot, twisting his empty glass against the palm of his hand, carried on, 'No, it's true. The speech this morning was less than gracious, I grant you. But as you've said yourself, that was for public consumption. Privately he has often asked me about your interests, your education. I really believe he appreciates and admires what you do here. And speaking of that,' he said, looking up from the glass in his hand and assuming a brighter expression, 'let's change the topic from court politics. Tell me what you've been up to this last week. Last time we talked you said something about planning to have a root around in the old palace in Jamner.'

'Goodness, I'd quite forgotten. I haven't had a chance to tell you!' Constable, his mood already transformed by his friend's assurance, was now visibly excited. 'I've made a major discovery! There's an old storeroom above the entrance gate into the garden courtyard. I got some workmen to break the locks, and found it full of the most magnificent carpets.'

'Really? Like the old Persian ones in the City Palace?' Talbot was clearly impressed.

'Like them, yes. Only they're not Persian. None of them are. My discovery throws light on their real origin.'

'I thought that they were supposed to have been brought back from Kandahar in the time of Raja Udai Singh, during Akbar's reign.'

'Well, that's what Cooke said in his history of Bhanupur. Turns out to be utter rubbish,' Constable continued gleefully. 'Listen. One of the carpets I found has an irregular shape. But it exactly fits the apartment known as the Kanch Mandir. That means it must have been made to order, for that room. But the room was built by Raja Vir Singh I, the contemporary of Shah

Jahan. That's long after Udai Singh and his Kandahar campaign. Also, and this is the key point,'—Constable here picked up and replaced his glass on the table for emphasis—'some of them have still got the maker's tags attached. They clearly state the place of production as Lahore. The conclusion is obvious.' Constable paused to allow Talbot to draw the inference for himself.

'What? That the whole lot were manufactured in Lahore?'

'More than that,' Constable resumed impatiently. 'That they were a bulk order. Vir Singh was able to commission them from the Mughal imperial workshops, and had them made to fit the rooms of the Jamner palace.'

'Well I suppose that does follow,' Talbot conceded, trying to conceal any doubt in his voice.

'Oh, Talbot! They are magnificent! True works of art!'

'And what do you plan to do with them, Constable? If I know you, the discovery is not the end of the matter. Do you have some plan about how to use them?'

'Well, first I have to conduct more thorough research into everything that is known about Indian carpets. But yes, in the long run we can use them as patterns to improve the quality of production in India today. I thought of proposing to the durbar to send one or two to somewhere like the jail in Agra. They have a carpet workshop to keep the prisoners occupied, you know. But the work done there is quite terrible. With something worthy of imitation in front of them . . .'

Constable was here interrupted by the yelping of a small dog, erupting through the veranda door and skidding across the floor towards Talbot's ankles. Talbot at last put down the empty glass he had held for so long and scooped the animal up in a large hand. But the dog was merely the harbinger of its mistress: it was soon followed by the slender figure of Mrs Talbot, stepping into the darkness. She crossed the threshold, with one hand held lightly against the edge of the closed leaf of the double door, and as she turned towards them, the light from the room within caught the ripples of silk that lay taut across her hips. The two men rose to their feet.

'Good evening, Richard. How nice to see you. And I must congratulate you on this morning. Your museum is'—she waved a hand—'a triumph. And you gave quite the best speech.' Constable began to mutter his thanks, but Mrs Talbot had already turned to her husband. 'Milton, dearest, if we are going to be on time for this banquet, you had better go and change, and let poor Richard here go home.'

The elegance with which Mrs Talbot ate soup was a marvel to Chatterjee. Covertly he studied it. The spoon held perfectly level and raised slowly to the lips; her straight back and slightly upturned chin making the journey an immeasurable distance: was all this the product of an art, taught perhaps in some academy in Kensington, or was it—as she made it appear—an entirely natural grace? He hardly wished to know the answer for fear of breaking the spell, but still he could not resist wondering. Certainly the action did more than justice to the comestible itself, billed as mulligatawny and frankly rather bland. It lent dignity, too, to the dingy environment of the banquet room. The light from the oil-filled chandeliers shone brightly enough on the crisp starched tablecloths and on the silverware heaped upon them, but could not penetrate the gloom of the carpeted floor or the lower walls—somewhat to the relief of Chatterjee, who was all too conscious of the patches of peeling paint in the nether regions.

The Khasa Kothi, the Maharaja's unofficial residence, lay outside the walled city, between the Ratan Niwas Gardens and the western suburb that was dominated by the bungalows of the European officials. The building belied its name, for it was in no way special, neither was it in any sense a private retreat. An uninspired neo-classical construction with a vast wing of identical guest rooms, it was used primarily for just such events as this, the entertainment of a distinguished European visitor. Some members of the Chief Commissioner's staff had even been accommodated in the guest wing, which functioned, to all intents and purposes, like a small hotel.

That was all well and good, in Chatterjee's view, as he generally learnt much about the visitors' thoughts and intentions from the bearers he personally appointed to serve them. But he regretted that for the main reception the Maharaja refused to use the old Banquet House built by his predecessor in the palace garden. That was a much grander structure, which better reflected the dignity and wealth of the state. There all the guests could be seated at a single table, eight feet broad and twenty feet long; while in the more confined space of the Khasa Kothi's dining hall it was necessary to have a T-shaped assembly that had the air of something makeshift. Of course, he fully understood the Maharaja's reservation. Serving wine, and employing a European chef (a German named Brücke) who could prepare continental dishes, were concessions the Maharaja was prepared and even glad to make in the interests of diplomacy; but staging the event in the palace garden—in such close proximity to the Madan Mohan temple—was repugnant to him. There he drew the line. Chatterjee respected the scruple but doubted whether the guests always believed the excuse he was deputed to offer them, that holding the dinner in the Khasa Kothi was intended for their own convenience, obviating the need for them to travel through the old city.

This evening, as always, a strict protocol governed the placement of the diners. Presiding at the centre, the Maharaja sat between his two principal guests, Sir Edward and Lady Grayson. Around them, on the arms of the T, were ranged the members of the Chief Commissioner's staff, the Resident, and the leading court nobles or Senior

Sardars. The supporting table, the stem of the T, was occupied by officers of the Mahakma Khas, the Maharaja's private office, and the European employees of the state, including Constable and Talbot. At the foot of this table, facing the Maharaja, Chatterjee sat surveying them all, with Mrs Talbot to his right. Had things been otherwise it should have been the Resident's wife in that place, but—as yet—there was no such person. Chatterjee rejoiced in Dr Hutton's bachelorhood almost as much as the Resident himself lamented it, affording him as it did opportunities such as this to talk to Mrs Talbot at length.

He had earlier greeted her in the European manner, wishing her good evening and extending a hand, and she had taken it in both of her own and smiled as she exclaimed warmly, 'Mr Chatterjee! Always a pleasure!', and had been happy to be led to her place at his side. Her teeth shone in the light from the chandeliers even more brightly than the pearls that hung around her neck.

'I do hope that you were not uncomfortable at this morning's ceremony,' he had said when they were settled. 'I fear it may have been rather hot for the time of year.'

'Not one bit! You need have no concern on my account,' she had assured him. 'I'm quite accustomed to the climate, as you know. Besides, the entire veranda was in the shade.'

'Ah! Because it is north-facing. We have to thank your husband's ingenuity for that convenience, as for many others.'

'I'm quite sure, Mr Chatterjee, my husband is not the first architect to think of making a building face north!' And she had smiled again, in light mockery, to deflect the compliment.

And now, as they exchanged comments on the museum display over the tepid plates of soup, he considered her movements, some studied and controlled, like the act of eating, some spontaneous and unconscious, as when she flicked a dark looping curl on her pale forehead, changing the line of its shadow.

Chatterjee was able to assure himself that there was nothing licentious in his admiration. He was wont to observe her just as he might any other of God's creatures— a demoiselle crane, perhaps—with the exception that despite the number of times they had met she always seemed surprising and unfamiliar. He wondered about this. European women in general presented something of an enigma to him; Mrs Talbot in particular, only because she was the specimen he had examined most closely. The enigma was the contradictory nature of their sexuality. The cut of the dress revealed so much, of shoulder and bosom, but these exposed portions seemed at the same time shrouded or protected by an invisible force, more impenetrable than any garment. He could only think of calling it bodily pride. It was all in the movement and the posture: however much might apparently be on display, a European woman prohibited touch by her deportment alone. But, then again, if the reserve was something performed, so too was their sensuality behavioural, something *done*. It seemed to Chatterjee that an Indian woman's sensuality was of a quite different kind, more intrinsic to the body. He knew (though he hardly dare state this even to himself) that an Indian woman's body could be sensual even in death, because it was a quality of the flesh itself. A European woman, he guessed, would in death appear nothing but lifeless, like a dropped puppet.

Chatterjee made use of occasions such as this evening to explore this mystery in the light of what he knew, or could discover, about Mrs Talbot as an individual, hoping that complete acquaintance with a specific would unlock the general case. To begin with, he knew her Christian name. Stephanie. Slight as it may seem on the surface, he counted this knowledge a great secret, because he knew he could never use it to address her, or even to refer to her. More importantly, he knew her private pain, for he had seen the pathetic, tiny grave in All Saint's churchyard, and he wondered, as she spoke, how close this image was to her conscious mind, working always to present a clear brow and a cheerful demeanour.

'I did very much like the miniature paintings,' she was saying. 'They depict a way of life so very different from our own. All that lounging about on immaculate terraces, listening to music and taking paan. It seems a world away, and yet they are not very old. Not from a long time ago, I mean. Less than a hundred years, some of them. Are they from the Maharaja's private collection, do you know, Mr Chatterjee?'

She knew herself to be under close scrutiny, but did not mind it. Not from Mr Chatterjee. Even when he seemed to be staring at her pearls, or at her fingers on the stem of her glass, it did not strike her in any offensive way. Well accustomed to male regard, she had learnt to distinguish lust from more innocuous kinds of glance, and she had long since marked Mr Chatterjee down as 'clean', though she had yet to fathom the real nature of his interest in her. Talbot sometimes teased her about her 'admirer', and she detected a note of jealous protection in his comments, but she did little to assuage his anxiety—referring to the prime minister privately as '*my* Mr Chatterjee'. Besides, she felt sure her husband's suspicions were unfounded.

Stephanie Talbot had quite simply decided to like Mr Chatterjee. His constant sweating, no doubt, undermined to some degree the dignity of the man, but it was a feature—once the decision to like him had been taken—that became one of the characteristic and, therefore, likeable things about him. It was true, too, that he often seemed rather earnest and too eager to please. His solicitude about her comfort, his comment about how pleased he was that she could grace this too-male occasion with her presence: such seemingly clumsy attempts at gallantry might have made her impatient. But she believed that at some level his chivalry carried an element of play-acting, that it was not fully sincere. And she liked him the better for this hint of charade. It suggested to her that he had a sense of irony.

He was answering her question about the miniatures, loyally stressing the Maharaja's generosity in parting with them for the benefit of the museum. Half involuntarily she turned to her right to consider the subject of these comments. The Maharaja was sitting quite still and not eating. It was his custom at these banquets to preside without partaking of the meal, and it was one of Chatterjee's many tasks to explain to guests in advance that His Highness would not break the caste taboo by sharing the meal he offered them. Mrs Talbot knew this, and she knew too that it embarrassed Chatterjee, so the Maharaja's refusal to eat was off limits as a topic of conversation.

It seemed that the host had also exhausted the stock of pleasantries he had prepared for his principal guests, for both had already turned their attention to their other neighbours. To his left, Sir Edward was talking earnestly to an elderly noble Mrs Talbot did not recognize, hectoring him, and receiving by way of response a series of vigorous nods of assent which signalled at once polite respect and a clear readiness to forget whatever was being said. Lady Grayson, meanwhile, looked more happily engaged with the young Thakur of Balgru. A clever piece of seating, in Mrs Talbot's view: this young noble, who was all of—what?—twenty years of age, was strikingly

handsome and was always ready with a good fund of
apposite topics. Between these two animated scenes the
Maharaja sat solid and silent, with an unfocused stare,
rapt in thought. His outline and expression reminded
Mrs Talbot of a statue of the enthroned Buddha she
had seen in the Ajanta caves. But was the Buddha ever
depicted with beard and turban? She thought not. She
would ask Richard Constable. He'd be sure to know.

The thought led her gaze to where Constable himself,
closer at hand, was talking across the table to her
husband. From a phrase she caught about wool dyeing
she surmised he was still on about his recent discovery
of a cache of carpets. Talbot had mentioned this find to
her on their way to the banquet. He really was the most
patient listener, she thought fondly, showing unfeigned
interest in all of the doctor's projects and passions.

'Most generous of him, indeed yes,' she said,
returning to her companion's last remark. 'Of course,
Dr Constable longs to see the Rudra-nama again. Isn't
that what it's called? The manuscript that His Highness
lent to the Exhibition. Personally I prefer the lovely court
scenes, so bright and detailed! Even if some of them are
a little exotic.'

Chatterjee blushed. He gave himself a pause, partly to
enable him to restart the conversation on a matter that
was on his mind.

'Mrs Talbot, please permit me to tell you how pleased
the durbar is about all the design work that your husband

and his staff have been taking on recently. I don't mean
only the Jubilee Hall, excellent though it undoubtedly
is. I understand they have also lately supplied designs for
some new buildings for the University of Allahabad and
many other public works. What was once our humble
state engineer's office is now the leading architectural
practice in the region. This can only enhance the
prestige of Bhanupur. And it is splendid news for local
employment. I gather Colonel Talbot has already taken
on several draughtsmen from our own School of Art.'

'I am certain that the Colonel would be delighted by
your approval, prime minister. But surely you could tell
him this yourself.'

'Oh, I do, I do tell him! And I must have another
talk with him about architecture soon. Just recently His
Highness and I have been debating the possibility of
putting up a new reception hall, a place for receiving
our distinguished visitors—such as Sir Edward—within
the palace precincts. Not quite inside the palace itself, I
should say. There is a courtyard a little distance inside the
Tripolia Gate, between the observatory and the court of
audience. That would be the ideal location, I think.'

'You forget, Mr Chatterjee, I'm not at all familiar
with the layout of the palace, as my husband is. We were
invited a number of times to the Banquet House in the
garden, during late His Highness's reign. That is as much
as I have seen of it. The palace garden always looked
so lovely, with the fountains playing and the temple lit

up like a fairy castle. If the Maharaja wishes to receive guests closer to the palace, why does he not use the Banquet House?'

'Ah, His Highness considers the Banquet House too large and pretentious,' Chatterjee answered smoothly. 'And it is rather old-fashioned. Something more convenient is required.'

Mrs Talbot caught his eye. 'I think I detect,' she said archly, 'that this is *your* project, not the Maharaja's. *He* dislikes the Banquet House, but *you* dislike the Khasa Kothi. Am I right?'

Chatterjee grinned conspiratorially. He leaned forward, hunching his shoulders and spreading his fingers on the tablecloth. He half-whispered, 'Do you?'

'What? Like the Khasa Kothi?' she smiled back at him. 'I grant you it's not the city's most distinguished building. But you always point out how convenient it is for us all, being nearer to our bungalows. But anyway, what has all this to do with my husband? Surely for a building in the palace grounds you would engage the Maharaja's official architect. I forget his name . . .'

'Banwari Lal,' Chatterjee supplied. 'Yes, Lalji is certainly an accomplished designer, but he does not have a monopoly on palace works. I would value the Colonel's advice on this matter. You know, he has already helped us out considerably with the late Maharaja's cenotaph, and he supervised all the artists redecorating the Dilkushal Mahal.'

'But you were not able to use him for the apartments that I understand His Highness has built inside that fort on the hill above the city—oh, what's it called?—Vijaygarh. My husband told me that, as palace buildings, they come under a different department.'

'Well, it was not only that.' Chatterjee was uncomfortably aware that he had been cornered by one of his own earlier diplomatic excuses. 'The rooms in Vijaygarh are of a traditional sort, primarily for the use of ladies of the court . . . there are special requirements . . . ' He trailed off.

'Miniature painting activities?' she asked slyly.

'Meaning?'

She laughed. 'Meaning nothing at all, prime minister. I'm being naughty. Please ignore me!'

There was a disturbance in Gota Bazaar. The traders who had their shops on this street, who included some of the city's leading cloth merchants as well as the longer-established silversmiths, had been growing increasingly indignant over the past several days about the condition of the main drain.

Put simply, it was blocked. Water ran in rivulets and collected in pools at an ever-increasing number of spots along the roadway, and even lapped at the steps of the long shared veranda that stretched in front of their shops. When the problem became apparent, some labourers carrying out a task for the public-works department were conveniently at hand to complain to. But they expressed no interest in effecting any remedy without properly channelled instructions. And then a little investigation by one or two of the traders revealed that it was the labourers themselves who had caused the problem. Instructed to rebuild the low perimeter wall of a temple that fronted the street, they had casually thrown rubble into the drain, as the nearest available ditch. When their error was pointed out to them, they continued to show indifference. This was *sarkari* work, they said, and if the *babu-log* had problems with it they should direct their complaints to the durbar. In any case, they could not possibly alter anything they were doing without orders from above. Until told otherwise, their concern was the wall, not the flood.

This riposte provoked a reaction that was as close to a riot as can be managed by a few dozen prosperous tradesmen whose greater interest was to ensure the free movement of customers towards their products. They gathered in groups and held up the traffic—those few vehicles that were still managing to negotiate the puddles— and exhorted everyone to join them in haranguing the labourers. Some tried to reason with them, pointing out alternative spots where they could discard the rubble; others resorted to obscenities, believing such language more likely to persuade.

But one among the silversmiths, Kansi Ram Tholia— whose shop in the lower-lying portion of the street was the worst affected—decided to take the labourers' advice and sent his peon with a note to the office of the public-works department in Naya Mahal. He had stepped into the inundated veranda to point out to the man where exactly to go. He then returned to his shop, stationed himself on his *gaddi*, and assumed an air of removal from the problem, telling agitated neighbours and colleagues that he had already done what was needful and that for a solution they merely had to wait and watch.

Even Kansi Ram was surprised though when, an hour later, Talbot turned up in person. He knew that, as director of the department, Talbot would have been quickly apprised of the situation. But he had expected the Colonel Sahib to send one of his assistants—someone like Ibrahim Hussain—to make an assessment on the ground, and he had privately entertained mixed feelings about the reception that such a minion was likely to receive, given the mood of his fellow traders.

The appearance of Talbot changed everything at a stroke. Kansi Ram rushed out of his shop and, ignoring the shouts of acclaim directed towards him—for his peon was widely advertising the success of his mission—approached Talbot as rapidly as his portly build permitted, offering profound regrets for having upset the department's schedule. Talbot genially brushed aside the apology:

'What nonsense, Tholia-ji. It was your duty to inform us of this problem. And I would happily have come here just for the honour of meeting you again. It has been a while since we have had the pleasure, has it not?'

Talbot publicly admonished his labourers, not so far as to humiliate them but enough to satisfy his larger audience. He told the workers that a merciful God had endowed them with brains as well as hands and that they must learn to use both, and he repeated, officially, the advice still being advanced volubly by one of the more excited traders, that they could for the time being store the rubble on an unused portion of pavement instead of in the drain. With the matter clearly set on a path towards resolution, he then graciously accepted Kansi Ram's invitation to partake of a cup of tea.

Later, as he sat awkwardly cross-legged in the silversmith's little shop, sipping sweet tea from a glass, Talbot remembered—and mentioned—his wife's insistence that he should pick up a little silver mug, for his regular early-morning drink of milk. Kansi Ram responded with alacrity, and as Talbot turned a simply-formed, finely-crafted beaker in his hand, pivoting it on his thumb, allowing the light to catch the delicately incised decoration, it occurred to him belatedly that Kansi Ram might embarrass him by offering it as a gift—might even assume that he was asking for one. There were ways, he thought, of refusing such offers, but he was not convinced in his own mind that he always managed those refusals with the same dignity that he felt he had just resolved the matter of the drain.

Despite this momentary anxiety, Talbot suddenly felt a surge of warmth towards Kansi Ram Tholia and his shop, towards Gota Bazaar, indeed towards the whole city of Bhanupur, his working environment. He believed himself lucky to be where he was, but did not consider himself the architect of his own good fortune. What quirk of fate, he wondered, what throw of the dice, directs us down particular paths? Descended from a long line of soldiers and East India Company servants, he was destined from birth, no doubt, for an Indian career. But chance—decisions made for the short term and mostly by other people—had taken him first from the army to the Bengal public-works department, and from there to his first assignment in Aden, where he had become a specialist in irrigation and drought relief. And then suddenly to Bhanupur—this strange realm which, as a Princely State, was not really a part of the British India he had known from childhood, but an annexe, an addendum.

That is how it had seemed at first, but after decades of service—and as it became apparent that his secondment was permanent, that he would spend his entire career here—he began, in his mind, to reverse the equation and to think of British India as the annexe (after all it was historically the later portion) and of the Princely States as India proper. These were thoughts he could not voice publicly. He shared them only with Constable, who seemed to feel them even more strongly. Such thoughts always left Talbot confused, and even as he wondered about their possible long-term effects on the people around him, he knew that he could not divulge them now, as he looked up, from the cup, into the still smiling face of Kansi Ram Tholia.

'I apologize for keeping you waiting, prime minister.'

Chatterjee had indeed been waiting for half an hour, and although comfortably seated in the deep veranda of the City Palace, he had come well prepared for his audience, with his portfolio by his side, and so had had little to think over or to rehearse to pass the time. He was gazing out across the palace garden towards the temple of Madan Mohan when a commotion within alerted him. He rose abruptly as the Maharaja bustled in, calling out his apology, and came to face him, still flustered, giving his explanation.

'I've been paying my respects at Bhagwat Singh's cenotaph, you know; and there was some problem with the carriage, that delayed my return. Sit, sit. What are you gaping at? Let's get on.'

Chatterjee had resumed his seat as instructed, but continued to look surprised.

'What's the matter with you, Panditji? Do you think it unseemly for a maharaja to apologize for being late?' And then, noting his minister's sustained silent stare, the Maharaja added, 'Ah, I see you cannot tactfully answer either yes or no, to that question. The British have a saying, I believe,'—he raised a finger—'punctuality is the courtesy of kings. The Resident told me that. I suppose he meant it as a reprimand. But I won't apologize to him. It's his job to wait on me. Yours too, but you have other work to do besides.'

Chatterjee remained silent a little longer, unsure how to respond, and then began cautiously, 'Forgive my impertinence, Sarkar. It was not your apology that surprised me, but the excuse.'

'What? That the carriage should break down? It happens every time I use it. What do you think, prime minister, could we get away with executing the Keeper of the Vehicles?'

'No, Your Highness, I do not. I trust you are in jest. But I wasn't referring to the difficulty with the carriage, of which I am all too well aware. I meant . . . the place that Your Highness said you were visiting.' Chatterjee stopped, and glanced towards the scarlet turban and white tunic of the attendant standing behind the Maharaja, causing the man to withdraw a step. He had not consciously intended that result, but no matter. His eye slid to the floor where a blade of sunlight cut diagonally across the carpet, highlighting the pile. He felt now in turn the Maharaja's silence bearing upon him, requiring him to explain. 'I had received some reports,' Chatterjee began again, 'that Your Highness had visited the Bhagwat Singh cenotaph. And I confess

I had supposed them to be mistaken, so I was surprised to hear of such a visit from your own lips. May I be permitted to enquire whether Your Highness intends to make this a regular practice?'

Chatterjee heard the Maharaja grunt and saw his eyebrows suddenly rise and quiver, like the surface of boiling milk. He braced himself for an outburst. But just as quickly the Maharaja's features subsided, as if the pan had been lifted from the flame.

'You *may* enquire,' the Maharaja replied gently. 'And I *do* so intend. What of it?'

'Sarkar, you must be aware that such a display of . . . partiality . . . towards that particular former ruler might . . . bear an odd construction. In certain quarters.'

'Certain quarters?' But the Maharaja seemed less inquisitorial, more amused, and he added, 'No, leave that aside. Let me ask instead, what construction? Answer me that, Panditji.'

'Your visits could be taken to suggest that you are willing to permit an association to be made in the people's minds between yourself and—forgive me for saying so—the least distinguished of your forebears. You must please make allowances for my being Bengali and an outsider here, Sarkar. But I am given to understand that Maharaja Bhagwat Singh died by his own hand.'

'That is so. Go on.'

'And that this accounts for the fact that he alone among the former Maharajas was not cremated at Sardar

Sagar. The separate placement of his cenotaph was intended to reflect the taint of his crime.'

'Yet it is closer to the palace than any of the others. Have you not thought of that? The royal cremation ground at Sardar Sagar lies outside the city walls, while Bhagwat Singh's cenotaph is within the palace grounds.'

The minister's confusion revealed that the point had not occurred to him, but also that it did not allay his discomfort.

'Let me help you out, and save you embarrassment, prime minister. I can, perhaps, put it more bluntly than you feel you are permitted. Among most of our citizens, and certainly among the nobles of the court, suicide is not considered a proper act for a Rajput king. It speaks of cowardice, and that is against our famous Rajput code. Countless generations of Rajputs have prized valour and dignity above all else, so that by comparison the despair of suicide is—as you call it—a crime. And now you fear the consequences to my personal reputation if I am seen to endorse such a crime by showing respect to one who has committed it. Do I have it about right?'

'Indeed, Sarkar, you express my concern most concisely. You are able, as you say, to speak more plainly on these matters than myself.'

'And to think more deeply on them, too, perhaps. For you know, Panditji, suicide is not in every case a sign of cowardice. Indeed, incidents of suicide also feature in the glorious annals of our Rajput race. Our womenfolk, in particular, have often willingly consigned themselves to the flames to avoid being captured and dishonoured by the enemy. Some say that in the fort of Chittor—even after hundreds of years—you can still smell the burning flesh of the wives of the Rajput heroes. They went willingly into the fire even before their husbands fell, to free the men from obligation and make them resist more fiercely. So they are honoured no less than the men. Rightly so. Self-sacrifice is sometimes the boldest and the hardest option.'

'And was Maharaja Bhagwat Singh's suicide of that nature, Sarkar?'

The Maharaja hesitated. 'Yes,' he replied, 'I believe it was. Not everyone would agree, I concede. But they have not considered the matter from the proper perspective—that of the Maharaja himself. Listen, Panditji, if your papers can wait a while,'—he waved a dismissive hand towards the prime minister's portfolio, still lying beside him—'then I will tell you about it.' Seeing by an inclination of the minister's head that he had his consent and attention, the Maharaja began his narrative. 'Bhagwat Singh died because of the ambitions of his brother.' He paused a moment, collecting his thoughts. 'But to explain that ambition one has to go back a step, perhaps. One might say that he died because of the folly of his father . . . on account of the terms of his treaty with Udaipur.' He stopped again. 'No, I can see that to tell it properly I must go still further back.' The Maharaja

leant back with raised hands, as if to indicate that the
sequence of events was now at his command.

'When the Mughal Emperor Aurangzeb died,' he
began again, 'there was a civil war between his sons for
the succession. Our own ruler, Vir Singh II, was at that
time in the service of one of the younger imperial princes,
Azam Shah, if I remember correctly. Custom and duty
bound him to support Azam Shah's claim, but it was a
hopeless case, and the legitimate heir, Bahadur Shah,
soon gained control. As a punishment for assisting the
rebel, Vir Singh was deprived of his kingdom. It was then
that he sought the aid of the Maharana of Udaipur, to
recover it. The Maharana was most obliging, in spite of
the old antagonism between our states. He even gave
Vir Singh one of his daughters in marriage, to seal the
alliance. But—and here was the rub—he insisted that any
son born of the union would be given precedence in the
succession here. This was against our customs but Vir
Singh readily agreed. He had no sons at that time, so no
one then living was put at a disadvantage. But things did
not turn out well for him. His first son died of a fever.
His eldest surviving son, who was Bhagwat Singh, was
the child of another queen. Many years later the Udaipur
queen gave birth to his third son, who was named Amar.
According to the treaty, Amar Singh should have been
adopted as Yuvraj, but Vir Singh had always intended
to ignore the agreement. He assigned some properties
to Amar Singh in compensation, and declared Bhagwat

as his heir. So when Vir Singh died, Bhagwat Singh was duly installed on the throne, and was recognized as the legitimate ruler even by the new Emperor.'

'And surely by the nobles, too,' the prime minister volunteered. 'This could not have been achieved without their consent.'

'Quite so, prime minister. I see you are not as ignorant of our laws as you pretend. But Amar Singh felt slighted and invoked the treaty. He was supported, of course, by the forces of Udaipur, and he even managed to persuade the Marathas to join his alliance. The war between the brothers raged for seven years. Seven years! Now, Bhagwat Singh was very well able to defend his position. He defeated his brother's supporters and their allies time after time. At one point he even erected the Bhagwat Stambha as a celebration of his victory. But as Amar Singh was his brother, and a son of Vir Singh, he always stopped short of having him killed. He had many opportunities to end the matter on the battlefield, and he might easily have had Amar Singh put to death by an assassin or a corrupted servant. But in honour of their father, he spared his life.'

'Such forbearance!' Chatterjee commented dryly.

'Well, for those times I believe it was.' The Maharaja smiled. 'Fratricide was not uncommon among the ruling families. We had not all learnt the benefits of mild Bengali manners. But you deflect me from my tale. The point is that Bhagwat Singh's mercy was wasted on Amar Singh who was persistent, never giving up his claim and always threatening further violence to achieve his objective. In time, Bhagwat Singh came to understand that the war was destroying the state. The treasury was bankrupt, and the involvement of the Marathas was ruinous, a political disaster that could only store up future problems . . . In the end he had to choose between himself and the state. He could continue to rule, but at the cost of Bhanupur's future. Or he could remove the burden by removing himself . . . . To allow Bhanupur to be ruled by his enemy was preferable to seeing it collapse altogether. And his enemy after all was no foreigner. Remember that Bhagwat Singh himself had no son, so if he had died in some other war or from disease then Amar Singh would have succeeded quite legitimately . . . So when his brother marshalled yet another force to attack the city, he gave the order that no resistance should be offered. Too many lives had already been spent. It required only one more. He told his chief minister of his resolve, and retired to his private apartments where he took his own life. When Amar Singh's forces reached the palace gates, the minister announced the Maharaja's death.'

Chatterjee was silent for a while at the conclusion of this story, and then remarked, 'So his suicide was not surrender, but the solution to a dilemma. Not despair, but strategy. And this is why you honour him, is that it?'

'He has been vilified by the historians, Panditji. You

know his name is not even mentioned in some of our genealogical charts. But he gave up his life for the benefit of the state quite as much as any of the old heroes of the battlefield.'

Chatterjee continued to be reflective. And then a thought struck him. 'Would Your Highness permit me to repeat this account?'

'What for? People know it well enough. Or they should do.'

'I mean, may I repeat it as an explanation to those who question the propriety of your visits to the cenotaph? I feel sure . . .'

'Certainly not,' the Maharaja replied abruptly. 'It is a private matter. I have told you only as my confidential adviser. If others choose to misconstrue my actions . . .'

'Hardly "choose", Your Highness.'

'Well, whatever their motives, they should learn to trust their ruler, and to think such things through for themselves. I will not coach them. Nor will I explain myself, or have you explain on my behalf. Let them think what they like. I will not be honouring Bhagwat Singh sincerely if I trumpet the reasons.'

Chatterjee frowned, and tilted his head in resignation. But there was another question on his mind. 'In view of this admiration for Maharaja Bhagwat Singh, Sarkar, it is a wonder that you should take the name of his rival as your own regnal name. I believe I am correct in saying that Amar Singh was not your given name at birth?'

'Indeed, that's right. My father named me Prahlad
Singh. When I was adopted the late Maharaja told me
that I would have to take another name when I succeeded
him. He said it should be the name of a former ruler,
so that I would at least sound more like a member of
the dynasty. In the event I had little time to choose. His
Highness died within eighteen months of adopting me.
I knew nothing then of the true story of Bhagwat Singh.
I learnt about it all later, from Pandit Madhusudan, who
was deputed to teach me the family history. At the time,
I decided to name myself after Amar Singh because he
was fat.'

Chatterjee's astonished face silently demanded
further explanation.

'Well, I couldn't have called myself after my adoptive
father,' the Maharaja continued wearily. 'Maharaja Ratan
Singh II was a truly great man, as everyone agreed . . .
both active and intellectual. He achieved so much for
Bhanupur. What everyone wanted when he died was
continuity. But if I'd become Ratan Singh III, everyone
would have compared us, and they would have said, "But
this man is no Ratan Singh. He hasn't got the brains."'

Chatterjee had stopped nodding his agreement and
began slowly to shake his head, but the Maharaja ignored
his responses. 'What all the world knows about Amar
Singh I,' he continued, 'is that he was fat. I don't mean
well fed, as a king should be. I mean obese. His portraits
show him as so large he could barely stand up. And so

I thought, people will only be able to say, "This new Maharaja is a fat man; but not so fat as his namesake." It was a comparison I came out better from.'

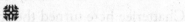

People had begun to gather before the Madan Mohan temple in readiness for the ceremony at noon. They were milling about, not yet focused on the still-shuttered shrine, some occasionally turning to face the palace, unaware that they were silently observed by the Maharaja and his minister, invisible in the shade of its veranda.

'So, let us do some work, Panditji. What have you got in your portfolio for me?'

The earlier conversation had taken the Maharaja's mind back to the start of his reign, a troubled period that he could now afford to reflect on whimsically. He enjoyed such moments of self-deprecation, partly because Chatterjee always looked so gratifyingly scandalized, but also, he told himself, because it was a good thing once in a while to recall the turn of chance, the seemingly random rotation of the wheel of fortune that had put him in his privileged position and had burdened him with duties. His demeanour now changed abruptly as he brought his attention to the job in hand, and he shifted in his seat to disperse the mood of reflection and to summon his powers of concentration.

Chatterjee untied the strings of his portfolio and extracted the top sheet. 'The first item is a letter from Sir

Edward,' he began in a brisk tone that acknowledged the change in his master. 'He thanks Your Highness for your hospitality and congratulates you on the opening of the museum. It is unnecessarily long, in his customary style'— Chatterjee here turned the sheet over to show that the Chief Commissioner had extended his comments onto the reverse—'but the sentiments are purely formal. I will file it in the usual way.' He wafted the letter dismissively and made as if to return it to his portfolio.

The Maharaja cut short this action by raising a hand, not to reach for the paper that had not been offered, but to demand a pause. 'Does he say anything specific about the museum?' he enquired gently.

'Only that he commends what he calls—where is it?—"the high quality and broad range of the display",' Chatterjee replied, looking again at the text, 'and he suggests that "it will play a significant role in public instruction in the city, and that it provides a model that is worthy of imitation in British India". I suspect he was fed these comments by Dr Constable.'

'Maybe so. But the letter might turn out to be useful all the same. Keep it by you. What is next?'

'A memorandum from Colonel Talbot,' Chatterjee said while pulling out a second sheet. 'He wants to propose to the durbar an addition to the irrigation works that are scheduled for the current year. You may recall, Sarkar, that we already have in progress some canal construction in the area on the west bank

of the River Bondi near Jamner, and in his proposed
submission the Colonel points out that while the work
is going on, it would be expedient to extend it further to
include a village called Dhani Nayan. It is an area that
has been greatly afflicted by drought in recent years,
and the extension of the canal and the construction of
a small embankment to create a tank would be a great
improvement and could easily be accomplished while
the adjacent work is progressing.'

'Easily, no doubt; but at what cost? What is his estimate?'

'Ah! As ever, the Colonel regrets that he is unable
to commit himself precisely on that until the work has
commenced. But he suggests the cost should fall between
ten and twenty thousand rupees.'

'And supposing we take the higher figure; can such a
sum be found within the existing budget for irrigation
works for the year?'

'No, Sarkar, not even the lower figure; the budget is
fully committed. But if the work is deferred to next year
the cost will increase because the workmen are available
now. And with the Jubilee Hall now complete we can be
sure of a saving in the buildings budget for the year, so
the added cost could be offset against that.'

'And this Dhani . . . what's it called? . . . Dhani Nayan:
is it a priority? Are you persuaded of the value of the
proposed work?'

'In terms of relieving hardship? Certainly. Or, at least,
I'm not really qualified to say, but I have complete trust

in Colonel Talbot's judgement in such matters. He's
usually right. In fact, he's never yet been wrong.'

'Then by all means allow his memorandum to be
forwarded to the members of the durbar for consideration
at our next meeting. And you might ask Colonel Talbot
if he could make himself available to attend . . . just in
case any other members prefer to trust his judgement
rather than yours.'

The satisfaction with which Chatterjee replaced the
memorandum in his portfolio indicated at once that the
decision was what he had hoped for, and his confidence
that what the durbar was invited to consider it generally
approved. 'Since we have brought up the matter of
Colonel Talbot's expertise,' he resumed in an off-hand
manner, as though a thought had just struck him, 'there
is a suggestion I've been wanting to put before you, if
I may, Sarkar, concerning another project that we've
discussed in the past, and on which we might profitably
engage the Colonel's advice.'

The Maharaja's raised eyebrows invited Chatterjee
to proceed while signalling that the casual tone had
not misled him into supposing that whatever was to
follow was unprepared, or out of sequence on the
minister's agenda.

'It's about the Khasa Kothi,' Chatterjee began,
meaning this statement to be confident, but conscious
that, in his own ears, it sounded more like a confession.
'I've mentioned before that I consider it in many ways

unsuitable for the reception of official guests. It lacks . . .
elegance.' Having sought for the appropriate word,
he wondered to himself why he had selected that
one. 'I understand—indeed I share—Your Highness's
reservations regarding the old Banquet House.' Here
he glanced into the garden, towards the point where
the offending building stood, though screened behind
trees; and he left it at that, as though the glance alone
were sufficient to indicate its proximity to where they
were sitting, as the chief among its many and grievous
faults. 'What is needed is some new building that is
convenient, easier for Your Highness to reach than
the Khasa Kothi, and in a style more commensurate
with the dignity of the state. This much I have said
before. Now, with your approval, Sarkar, I'd like to
seek Colonel Talbot's advice on where to place such
a building.'

'Why Colonel Talbot? Are you forgetting our own
court architect, who surely deserves to be considered for
any such commission?'

Cheered that the idea had apparently reached
the status of a commission in the Maharaja's mind,
Chatterjee was willing to concede a little ground.
'Banwari Lal undoubtedly has great talents, and when
we come to the designing of the building he must be
assigned some part to play. But Colonel Talbot has great
experience in planning; and he is also there to be used,
after all.'

'Before you run away with the idea that I have consented, prime minister, tell me first how we are to finance such a project.'

'Well, as I've mentioned, Sarkar, the completion of the Jubilee Hall is a great relief on the annual buildings budget . . .'

'Yes, but you've already spent that dividend at Dhani Nayan!'

'Only for the current year, Sarkar. The saving will be recurring, and there is no other major building project planned at present.'

'Very well, you may proceed. But slowly: I do not feel the urgency in this matter that you wish me to. And please remember that you can't use the completion of the Jubilee Hall as a justification for every one of your schemes. You can't spend the same saving twice, prime minister. In fact, I question whether we can properly call it a saving at all. The building costs for the Jubilee Hall became a fixed item in the annual budget only because it took such a confoundedly long time to finish. Its completion is certainly a relief but it's not strictly a saving. The costs were never planned to run for ever, you know, much as it might have seemed otherwise at times.'

Chatterjee looked satisfied. The lesson in economics was a small price to pay for the advance he had made. He had previously rehearsed in his mind what he would say to Talbot to gain his interest; indeed, he imagined that Talbot's curiosity should already be aroused if, as he had planned, Mrs Talbot had reported their conversation on the evening of the banquet. But as he extracted the next sheet of paper from his portfolio his face clouded, in recognition of the challenge it presented. 'I have next a letter from Dr Bose, the principal of the Maharaja's College, Sarkar. It comes with a full report on the College's recent development and current activities. It is an excellent document.' But he did not sound enthusiastic. He paused, and sighed.

'Why does this topic give you pain, Panditji?' The Maharaja smiled broadly. 'I thought you enjoyed your years working there, before I plucked you out for high office?'

'It is just because I enjoyed those years—and because I sympathize with Dr Bose's ambitions for the College—that I am troubled. I do not see a way towards their fulfilment.'

'What is it that he asks for?'

'In short, to be permitted to teach bachelor degrees.' He stopped again, as if the bald statement alone revealed the utter hopelessness of the case.

'You had better explain, Panditji. As you know, I am not generally reckoned an expert in matters of education.'

Having extracted an embroidered handkerchief from the folds of his clothing, Chatterjee wiped his forehead and dabbed his cheeks. His tone, in resuming, was patient, even pedantic. 'When the College was founded by late His Highness, it had just forty pupils, divided between three classes, learning Sanskrit, Urdu and English. Today it has grown beyond recognition. There are over eight hundred pupils and they learn every subject you can imagine. Arithmetic and geometry, the natural sciences, history—everything! And at every level, from the junior classes right up to matriculation. But not beyond. If the brighter boys wish to go in for higher studies, they have to leave Bhanupur to join a university in British India. For most this is a deterrent. Even those families who can afford it cannot bear the separation. So having tasted learning they have to stop, and the best we can do for them is find them a desk in one of the administrative departments. I myself have had pupils who could contribute so much more, and so has Bose . . . ' He broke off and resumed the dabbing exercise before concluding, 'The obvious next step is to introduce BA degrees.'

'And what is the great obstacle to this "obvious" step?' The Maharaja was partly amused and partly indignant. This was not a suggestion he had even heard before, much less refused, but the matter was still not clear to him. 'Why should we not let them take their degrees here in Bhanupur itself?'

'We need an affiliation, Sarkar. We cannot simply announce that we will teach and award degrees, without reference to authorities outside. Our degrees would not be recognized; they will be considered worthless unless they are approved by a university in British India—Bombay or Calcutta, or perhaps Allahabad.'

'Of those options, I presume that your own preference would be for Calcutta . . . where you yourself graduated?'

'Not me alone. Bose. Half the staff of the College. It has always been so. If indeed we could secure an affiliation with Calcutta University it would strengthen the informal bond we have, and make it so much the easier for us to recruit the necessary new teachers.'

'You have still not explained to me, Panditji, why this cannot be done. Let us by all means affiliate our college to Calcutta University, if that will lend it greater credibility. Why should we not?'

'Because they will not give it.' Chatterjee, who had grown gradually more animated, suddenly became sullen. 'Resident after Resident has praised the College, and has expressed approval of its expansion. When they speak of the rapid rise of education in Bhanupur I do believe they are sincere—indeed, I think they imagine their praise and encouragement to be the main motivating force. They think we are doing it just to please them. But, even so, they want it to remain a school. Neither they nor the Government of India want to see the College take on the task of higher education. They don't want us breeding a class of intellectuals in a state like Bhanupur . . . . They won't say as much, of course, but it's the last thing they want. We're supposed to be traditional. They applaud when we emancipate ourselves, but we can advance only so far as is deemed safe. They're happy to admit some of our Bhanupur boys into their own universities where they can be taught the benefits of British rule. But a home-grown institute of learning in Bhanupur itself? That is not to be tolerated. They won't give this as the reason. If we apply for affiliation, it will be refused. But not on this ground. It will be said that we lack the necessary resources.'

'What resources? I thought you said that we could recruit the teachers from Calcutta?'

'The teachers, yes. But the books, the teaching materials, the classrooms—all will be judged inadequate. And, to be honest, Your Highness, I would have to admit, such a charge would be hard to rebut.' Chatterjee was now at his most solemn.

Without turning round the Maharaja beckoned the attendant, merely by curling the fingers on his raised right hand, and as the scarlet turban bent before him, ordered water to be brought. He considered Chatterjee's account of the British, and it rang true. This constant talk of progress, and claiming credit for promoting it . . . but always seeking to contain it. Their attitude to himself was similarly divided: he was expected to be a reformer and a traditionalist at the same time; both active and inert. And he was irritated by the thought that his efforts at compliance would be construed as toeing the line. For, in truth, precisely the same mixed demands were made upon him by his subjects. They too wanted a maharaja of the old style, but they also expected him to provide modern amenities, schools and hospitals. They demanded every new convenience but spoke proudly of those who had not abandoned the old ways. And why should they not? It was useless to point out the contradiction, even if a contradiction is what it really was. They were as they were, and it was his given task to be as they wished him to be. He played the game for them, and gladly, only troubled that the British might misconstrue his efforts as intended to appease themselves. So it was necessary sometimes to distinguish between the games, to play outside the British rules. Refusing to eat in their presence was one such move of his: as a gesture it was a little too orthodox for British manners to accept, but it delighted a conservative faction in the city's bazaars.

Being too progressive was not a tactic that he had as yet successfully achieved. An earlier attempt had met with failure. His legislation to cap the amount that could be spent on marriage parties had, to his dismay, been warmly welcomed by the British. But was condemned by some of his subjects who were among those worst hit by the tradition of excess. They said it offended their dignity. So the game was not without risk. Perhaps this question of upgrading the College could afford a safer opportunity.

The silent attendant reappeared with a silver tray and with immense care placed one tumbler of water on the

low table beside the Maharaja, and another in front of
the prime minister's fleshy outstretched hands.

'What about the Jubilee Hall?' the Maharaja asked
suddenly, when the man had returned to his station.

'What about it, Sarkar?' Chatterjee was flustered,
having lost the thread of the interrupted conversation.

'We have it on record,' the Maharaja began, adopting
something of Chatterjee's own patient manner of speech,
'that the Chief Commissioner himself believes that the
museum displays will contribute to education—indeed
that they offer a model for British India to imitate. Here
now is the use of his letter. It supports the claim we will
make that the Jubilee Hall is a unique resource. We
will conduct classes using its collections as the teaching
material. The central hall can be used for lectures. And
hasn't Dr Constable started a library on the top floor?'

Chatterjee nodded, but looked quizzical.

'It will probably need some improvement,' the
Maharaja continued. 'We might put there those books
on more technical subjects that are in the Public Library,
that are seldom used by the general population, and
establish a special category for student members of the
museum's library. We'll use what we have. Don't you see,
Panditji . . .? Sir Edward may have meant his comments
to be routine, but unwittingly they cut the ground from
under the objection that you expect to be made. Who
can say that we lack the necessary resources? The Chief
Commissioner himself has said otherwise!'

At last Chatterjee smiled. 'I'm sure he will be delighted
to find himself quoted. But . . . Sarkar, it may not be
enough.' He knew that the Maharaja was too well aware
of the need for caution to feel crestfallen at such a
warning, and that it would be taken as constructive. 'We
might strengthen the case if we could solicit a second
testimonial, from an authority less elevated but more
closely involved in education.'

'Does anyone come to mind?'

'We could ask the principal of Mayo College to write
a confidential report on education in Bhanupur. I forget
his name . . . Wellington, I think . . . anyway, he's an MA
in history from Cambridge. Of course there's a risk that
he'll try and be smart and write something critical and
so do more harm than good.'

'Then don't make it official,' the Maharaja countered.
'Invite him instead to spend part of his spring holidays
in Bhanupur as a guest of the state. We could put him
up in Khasa Kothi if you think it's—what was your
word—"elegant" enough for him? Tell him that we
are asking him so as to strengthen our links with his
esteemed establishment, and because we would value
his advice about how to improve the curriculum at our
own college. He'll be flattered. Anything he writes will
be positive.'

If Chatterjee disapproved of the implication of this
remark, he did not show it, and the concern he voiced
was not moral but tactical. 'Mr Wellington might

object to any unsanctioned use of such an informal testimonial, Sarkar.'

'He might. But he won't be able to retract it without looking a fool. Send him an invitation, Panditji, but I think you and I should keep the longer perspective to ourselves for the time being, until we have made further progress. By all means inform Dr Bose of this conversation, and thank him for his report, but advise him against canvassing other members of the durbar at this stage.'

These instructions for action seemed to signal the conclusion of the meeting and Chatterjee began to shuffle his papers back into his portfolio.

'Before you go, prime minister . . . I'm curious . . . .' His expression was genial as Chatterjee looked up. 'Curious as to why you are reluctant to let me read Sir Edward's letter for myself.'

'Reluctant, Sarkar?' But the air of innocence was too obviously feigned.

'Reluctant. You waved it about but did not pass it to me. Even now you are keeping it covered, I notice.'

Chatterjee fumbled for it. 'If Your Highness would like . . .'

'No, I wouldn't. But I'd like you to answer my question. What is in it that might offend?'

There was no alternative but to reveal what he had hoped to suppress. 'There is nothing directly offensive, Sarkar. It is merely an implication. Sir Edward . . . takes it upon himself to express the hope that . . . you will soon be blessed with an heir.'

'What possible offence could be inferred from such a sentiment?' But though the tone was still genial the Maharaja had stiffened, and his own charade of innocence was equally plainly false. He knew what the comment meant, and why Chatterjee had tried to keep it from him. 'These British!' he muttered. 'They even wish to dictate which women I sleep with!'

His mind travelled to Vijaygarh and to the solace he found there. How could he explain—*why* should he explain—to Sir Edward, to Chatterjee or to anyone else, the comfort those women gave him? It was not that his concubines had higher personal qualities than any of his legitimate wives. They were no more intelligent or gifted, even in the arts of love. He was no fonder of them nor were they of him. The same rivalries and jealousies divided them, and they were obsessed by the same scheming for his attention. But because they had so much less to gain they were artless about it. It was as if tradition required them to be scheming, but seeing no profit in it they played the expected role openly, in jest. Their play-acting both mirrored and mocked the stifling intrigue of the palace zenana. Their insincerity carried no deceit because it was declared. So Vijaygarh was his refuge, a place where he could divest himself—if only for an interval—of the mantle that had been thrust upon him by his adoption. Duty required that he produce a legitimate heir, and that obligation too, like all the others, he would face in time. But not yet.

'You say nothing, prime minister, though I think I can guess your mind.'

Chatterjee had indeed ventured no comment and now stared blankly back at him, refusing to be drawn. Not yet, he said to himself, unknowingly echoing the Maharaja's last thought. Not yet.

'Kashinathji!'

A distance of no more than sixty yards separated the office of the honorary curator, situated at the north-east corner of the Jubilee Hall, from the office of the museum's chief clerk in the symmetrically corresponding north-west. Yet Dr Constable managed to create such a commotion as he made this brief journey—along the building's front veranda, and across the central porch—calling out the chief clerk's name and flapping a piece of paper in his hand as he went, that a sweeper who had to dodge out of his path remarked to the assistant storekeeper standing by, that, 'The Doctor Sahib must be off to fight Ravan, he is in such a rage!'

Bursting through the brass-plated door of the chief clerk's office without pausing or knocking, Constable confronted the startled occupant with, 'Ah, there you are! Have you seen this preposterous document?' He knew even as he uttered it that neither part of this speech was quite reasonable. 'There you are' implied that Kashinath had been hard to find, when he had been found in the first and most obvious place to look. And the poor man could not possibly have seen the paper that Constable stood flourishing, as it had only a moment before been carried to Constable's desk by a courier who had come straight from the City Palace. Constable thrust the offending paper in front of his colleague and by gesture invited him to read it, but he began his commentary even before Kashinath had had a chance to begin.

'It is a letter,' he said, struggling to control his temper, 'from the estimable Babu Chatterjee—in reply to our request to know the views of the Maharaja about which of his predecessors should be included in the series of portraits that we plan to put up in the entrance porch of this building. It's absurd! I can't imagine what His Highness is thinking of!' He flung himself uninvited into the chair facing the clerk.

Kashinath perused the list of names of former maharajas, silently and nervously, his concentration distracted by Constable's continuing impatience, and at length looked up, nonplussed. 'What is wrong with it?' he asked innocently.

'What's wrong with it? Kashinath, you amaze me! The set of portraits is supposed to honour the most distinguished rulers. But it seems from this letter that the Maharaja does not wish to include Bhuvan Rai. The man who founded the state apparently does not merit inclusion in our hall of fame. But he does want us to include Bhagwat Singh, whose only notable action was to commit suicide! It makes a laughing stock of the whole idea.'

'How can that be, Doctor Sahib?' Kashinath asked, for the explanation had not lessened his puzzlement. 'Who will laugh?'

'Why, the good people of Bhanupur, of course. They will look for Bhuvan Rai and find him left out. And in his place the most unworthy . . .' Constable broke off in exasperation.

'I very much doubt that the general population's knowledge of our history is as detailed as your own, Doctor Sahib.' Kashinath's tone was at once reasonable and flattering. He knew that the fear was unfounded and that Constable himself would soon recognize it as such, but he also knew that irritation was not a mood that Constable relinquished easily. He could not afford to be dismissive, and persisted in the same vein. 'The people will see only portraits of maharajas in fine clothes, and they will believe them all to have been equally great men.'

Constable at once saw the truth of this. Indeed the point had already dimly occurred to him, but he had set it aside as a consolation for later. He was not yet ready to be soothed. 'They will see a legendary hero slighted,' he contended. 'They've all grown up with the stories of Bhuvan Rai and they will expect to find him here. Instead of which they will see a reminder of the ruling dynasty's shame. How do you account for the Maharaja's obsession with Bhagwat Singh?' he continued. 'I'm told he's been visiting Bhagwat Singh's cenotaph. Is that dignified?'

But these were not questions that Kashinath would have ventured to answer even if he had had information, which he did not. So he remained silent, and hid his gaze in the lines of the prime minister's letter, which he still held.

'Well, it's a mystery to me. A mystery,' Constable repeated, but he was quieter now, partly out of respect for his colleague's reticence, and partly because he was running out of steam. He contemplated Kashinath's solid frame and motionless bald head, and was left only with the frustration that arises from realizing that one's disapproval makes no impact. 'And I've no idea how it is to be done,' he objected, as a final foray. 'Is there any known picture of Bhagwat Singh that can be used as a model, for the artists to copy?'

'Ah, yes, Doctor Sahib!' Kashinath looked up brightly. 'There is a beautiful portrait of him in the City Palace. I am sure you must know it. It was made by the former court painter, Gopi Chand. It shows the Maharaja Sahib dressed quite simply, without ornaments, all in white! Do you not recall it?'

It was obvious that even if Constable could not, for the moment, recall the picture, Kashinath had it clearly present before his mind's eye; and as he listened to this speech, Constable was struck less by his own forgetfulness than by the chief clerk's face, suddenly illuminated by a look of surprise and wonder.

At the water's edge, the light winked. From a distance it was hard to make out whether it was sunlight sparkling on the rippled surface or the jerky movements of pale-bodied birds. Earlier, while they were climbing into the boat, Stephanie had noticed little flocks of stilts running about randomly at the lakeside. Trim, black-and-white bodies wobbling over improbably long pink legs that might have been coloured to match the city walls by some extravagant royal command. Looking back at the shore from the island palace, she could no longer be sure if those sparks of whiteness were birds or not. And for a moment, she felt oddly vexed by that. She really wanted to know, to be able to see clearly and understand and not to have to settle, or rest content with puzzling impressions in a strange land. Ah!—she would have liked to be able to say to some visitor less familiar with the place—those sparkles may look like sunlight on the water, but actually you know they are pretty little waders called stilts.

She clung briefly to the stout marble column and leaned out of the balcony to contemplate the water lapping at the palace wall beneath her feet. The room's open side allowed a full view of the lake and the encircling hills, and must once have been a soothing place to spend an hour or two. She tried to imagine herself as a princess in a miniature painting, but the room did not assist her, with its pigeon mess and dust proclaiming its long disuse.

The adjoining rooms were similar in form and were strung along the same line. She wandered through them, listlessly at first and then with more determination, to find that all of the apartments were lined along the outer edges of the square, always looking out over the water, never leading inwards towards the island's core. The inner wall of every room had no doors, only filled-up arches. So what was in the centre, she wondered? Could it be solid? Were there concealed apartments that could not now be reached? Every now and then between two rooms she came across an arch that opened to a stone staircase, leading down into darkness. But she did not venture down one, fearing she would soon lose her sense of direction, that her cries for help would go unheard.

As it was, she knew that the line of empty rooms must eventually bring her back to her starting point, to the broad steps leading up on to the roof garden, where Richard Constable and her husband had gone on ahead. She found them lounging in one of the side pavilions, smoking their pipes and issuing redundant instructions to the servants struggling with hampers and a trestle table. And she sank with an exaggerated sigh into the chair between them, while unpinning her hat with lifted arms.

'Find anything interesting down below?' her husband asked genially enough, but with a tone that implied he knew that she had wasted her time by insisting on exploring.

'Actually, you are right, it's rather nicer up here. Though the garden could do with some attention.'

The men followed her gaze across the bleached terraces of the formal garden. Little of the original structure remained—just some pieces of curb and railing, a broken fountain, and the outline of a pool. The shrubs had become overgrown and the saplings of neem, to judge by their irregular positions, must have been self-seeded.

'Still, I'm glad to have seen it,' she added, sounding too defensive she thought. 'It is wonderful, but oddly disturbing, in a medieval sort of way, don't you think? Is it known when it was actually built?'

'I seem to remember reading somewhere that it was built for Maharaja Karan Singh,' her husband replied. 'Same fellow who built the Jhanki Mahal. So that would make it at the most a hundred years old. Seventeen-eighties. Something like that. Hardly medieval, dear.'

'You probably read that in Cooke,' Constable interjected, as if awaking from a reverie, and slowly, creating the uneasy feeling in his listeners' minds that he was ordering his thoughts for a longer speech. 'And like most of what Cooke has to say on matters of architecture or archaeology, it's utter tosh,' he pursued, confirming their fears. 'For one thing, the building's mentioned in the description of Bhanupur by Father Valignano, and that was written during the reign of Bhagwat Singh who—as I have recently had unfortunate occasion to recall—died by his own hand in 1750. For another thing, it is mentioned in a document relating to the seventeen-thirties. I owe that little discovery, I have to admit, to our egregious friend Chatterjee. He recently sent me a bundle of old documents which he felt would be more suitably kept in the museum than in his office stores. I must say I commend him for that bit of good sense. Anyway, one of them turned out to be a sort of account book or ledger that includes records of payments for the building of a "Jahaz Mahal" in the early seventeen-thirties. Well, the Jahaz Mahal referred to must be this one—it is still known by that name. So your guess is out by about fifty years, Talbot. It's still not "medieval", I grant you. Whatever made you think *that?*'

The last phrase was directed with more force than the speaker had meant towards Stephanie, who was, however, unruffled by the challenge and replied with a smile, 'I probably use the term more loosely than you would allow, Richard. I was trying to describe the building's character more than its date. It was a feeling it gave me.'

And she smiled again as she observed Constable looking baffled, and struggling to suppress his impatience.

Any embarrassment was averted by the soft approach of the bearer who offered a meek namaste to Talbot by way of signalling that their lunch was ready. Talbot

responded with a nod and a single raised podgy finger,
but none of them moved.

'And what was it built *for*, do you suppose, Richard?'
Stephanie resumed. 'All of the rooms below have
lovely views, but that's all they seem to have. It's as though
the whole place was built just for sitting and looking
at the lake.'

'That's about it, I should say,' Constable replied more
encouragingly. 'It's for spending a lazy afternoon enjoying
a picnic amid beautiful scenery, just as we are doing now . . .
by courtesy of the Maharaja. It's rather decent of him—
don't you think—to open it up and let us in?'

'Does he never use it himself? He must like to come
here sometimes.'

'One suspects he has other diversions, when he can
afford the time. And not down here but up on that hilltop,'
and he jabbed the stem of his pipe at the skyline.

'Oh, Constable!' Talbot interjected, 'Let's not lower
the tone by getting into bazaar gossip.'

But Stephanie wanted to pursue the topic. 'No, do
tell me about Vijaygarh,' she insisted. 'I don't suppose
either of you has ever visited it, but do we know what
really goes on up there? It's always mentioned as some
sort of school for scandal.'

'It is known only,' Talbot began with slow and deliberate
enunciation, hoping to keep the matter brief, 'that he
lodges there a number of concubines who for reasons

of their status cannot reside in the zenana. It's pretty unsavoury, but after all it's the man's private business.'

Talbot had only a slender hope that this speech would satisfy his wife's curiosity, but he was still surprised when she replied, 'Milton, dearest, do you think that if you were a maharaja you would keep a large harem?'

He tried to look amused. 'I'm not sure that I'm cut out for the role of oriental despot . . . and certainly not for polygamy. What exactly are you driving at, Steph?'

'Oh . . .' she shrugged, trying to sound vague, as though it were merely a passing thought. 'I just wonder whether custom and habit make us seem more different than we really are. The Maharaja is not a monster, after all. And if one were brought up with different codes of behaviour, they would no doubt seem perfectly natural.' And then to avert any serious discussion, she added more lightly, 'I think you would make a splendid maharaja, Milton . . . and I rather fancy I would enjoy life as an Indian princess.'

'You would be bored out of your mind within a week,' her husband announced emphatically, as if to declare the subject closed.

But still she persisted. 'I'm sure there must be a practical reason for polygamy, at least originally. We tend to think of harems as places of . . . voluptuous idleness . . . with perfumed fountains and all that. But I can't help thinking that we have got that idea from our own poets, not from theirs. They probably have a much more down-to-earth view of it. Having lots of wives must once have been about securing alliances and ensuring the dynastic succession.'

'Well, the system has signally failed our great Maharaja on that score,' Constable retorted, seizing on a solitary matter of certainty in this discussion, which seemed to him to lack intellectual bearings. A lack of firmness in first principles was a trait that he always found frustrating in partners in conversation, and although he was inclined to be more indulgent towards women, he had been unsettled by this notion of hers that differences of custom counted for little, that if circumstances were otherwise, we each might be capable of living other lives. But her last comment was easy to rebut, and he added brutally, 'With castles full of women, he still has no heir.'

'You are both rather wide of the mark, if I may say so,' Talbot interrupted judiciously, 'because, as you probably know, sons born to concubines can't inherit the throne.'

'Yes, but I've never understood why that is so,' Stephanie protested. 'Maharajas are allowed to adopt, aren't they, if they don't have a son of their own. Our Maharaja himself was adopted. So why can't he just adopt a son born to one of his concubines?'

'Well, that's just contrary to their customs,' Talbot replied. 'If the mother is not legally married, her son will be illegitimate. Whereas, a boy who is adopted from outside is at least a legitimate child, even if he's someone else's.'

'It seems a little harsh,' she observed sympathetically. 'I mean, a concubine's boy might grow up to be a decent fellow and a capable ruler. Imagine what it would be like having to watch someone else take your place! It seems so unfair. It's not as though there would be any doubt about the paternity, since the women are kept locked up in the fort. Any hint of misdemeanour on their part and I expect they get thrown to the crocodiles. Oh, that reminds me . . . Mr Chatterjee told me that there are crocodiles in the lake—is that true?'

Both men looked relieved by this distraction.

'Why don't we go and see if we can spot them?' Talbot suggested. He rose from his chair and gestured to the others to follow him to the railing that ran along the southern edge of the garden. Passing their lunch table, he extracted a chicken drumstick from a brass tureen, clenched it between thumb and forefinger, and on reaching the parapet pitched it with a vigorous jerk into the water below. They watched the tiny plop, half expecting an immediate swish and swirl of snout and scaly back beneath the surface. But there was only stillness.

Talbot chuckled and squinted, facing the sunlight. And then he silently pointed to the middle distance, at a spreading rippling pattern, not below but just above the surface, made not by crocodiles but a flock of sandpipers changing their course as they skimmed low over the water.

1902

1902

'*O*m, *bhur bhuvah svah!*' intoned Pandit Haridas sonorously, and then, leafing through the manuscript lying on his lap, somewhat vaguely added '*tatsavitur . . .*' before trailing off.

The Maharaja glanced across at him, wondering whether the pandit had lost his place and was reverting to the Gayatri Mahamantra as a stop-gap. They sat cross-legged on a dhurrie with a group of assistants, closely packed on a stone-paved platform by the side of Apollo Bunder. A flight of broad steps led down into the sea. In front of them a frame of plantain fronds made a sort of window overlooking the water. Above and behind them the footpath of the quay thronged with spectators. Some were members of the Maharaja's party but most were passers-by, jostling for space at the parapet to see what was going on. Beyond this surging crowd rose the grey-and-white facade of the new Taj Mahal hotel—still in the process of construction and partly obscured by a wooden cage of scaffolding—but already pimpled with ornate balconies and raising its red roofs and domes against the bright May morning sky.

The noisy enthusiasm of the audience in no way distracted the participants on the platform below, but it lent their ceremony an informal air that covered the pandit's hesitations. The ritual was indeed unfamiliar. The Samudra Pujan, or worship of the ocean, was not one that he had performed before, or was ever likely to again. The textual references he had found were not all consistent and he had stitched together a plausible order of ceremony from more than one source. Getting back into the rhythm that he had rehearsed, he now recited the verses more fluently.

The Maharaja watched him indulgently. He admired the seriousness of Haridas and was glad that this episode in his reign had afforded the pandit an opportunity to prove his worth. Understanding only half of what he heard, he was happy to let the pandit take the lead, and to await the signal for his own allotted part.

It seemed marvellous to him that they should now be enacting just what Chatterjee had ingeniously suggested many months before, turning embarrassment into triumph. He recalled the meeting the previous autumn, when the Resident, Mr Crabbe, had called at the City Palace with an invitation to the Maharaja to attend the coronation in London of the new King Emperor, Edward VII. Having announced in advance only that he had a personal message to deliver from the Emperor,

Mr Crabbe was summoned and met with due ceremony.
The occasion was all the more welcome as it provided
an opportunity to inaugurate the recently completed
Jalsa Ghar, the exquisite pavilion that Banwari Lal had
constructed in the outer courtyard of the palace. The
Maharaja was glad that he had given way to Chatterjee
over the need for such a building, but equally pleased with
himself that he had insisted that Banwari Lal should be
entrusted with its design. He conceived it as a place that
would provide a splendid welcome while keeping at bay
the casteless overlords. And, with that purpose in mind,
it would hardly be appropriate for it to be considered as
the work of an Englishman. Colonel Talbot, it was true,
had been in Bhanupur for so long that he was practically
a member of the court, and the Maharaja was to rely on
him for other services now in connection with the voyage.
But much as he liked Talbot personally, he knew that
the British would see his involvement in the building as
another little British victory, a further encroachment into
the affairs of the palace, and he wanted his pavilion—if he
was to have one at all—to bear a different meaning. How
fitting that a personal message from the Emperor himself
was to be received in surroundings that even Chatterjee
would deem elegant; but on the threshold of the palace,
away from his unpolluted halls of power.

When Mr Crabbe read the letter aloud, before an
assembly of selected ministers and thakurs, and it became
clear that it was more than a conventional message

refreshing the bonds of allegiance, that it included an invitation to visit London to attend the coronation, the Maharaja feared he had miscalculated. He saw at once the dilemma it posed. It was an honour that reflected the importance accorded to Bhanupur, and as such was to be celebrated. But how could he accept an invitation that required him to cross the sea and lose caste? Having made a public virtue of his orthodoxy, he could not be seen to abandon so fundamental a principle. A refusal would throw away the advantage gained, but an acceptance would make him look ridiculous in the eyes of his subjects.

He scrutinized the Resident's features for signs that Crabbe himself perceived the challenge that his message contained. Indeed, he wondered whether Crabbe's masters had intended it. Affronted, as he meant them to be, by his determination to keep his distance from them, had they exploited this chance to turn his orthodoxy against him? Given time, there would be ways to find that out, and ways to learn, too, whether Crabbe shared in the conspiracy or whether he could be trusted to help find a solution. For the moment, the Maharaja could do nothing but acknowledge the honour while adding, 'Since this matter concerns our state, and not myself alone, you will understand, sir, that we are bound to refer it to the durbar.'

As the Resident nodded in agreement with a knowing smile, the Maharaja graciously thanked him for delivering the message expeditiously, in a tone that might have been taken to imply that he regarded the Resident's role as that of a mere postman.

Once the Resident had departed, the assembly seemed mildly surprised at being dismissed before the Maharaja had left the room, though some might have guessed that he wanted an immediate confidential talk with Chatterjee. Left alone, the two men rose from where they sat and began to pace about within the ring of gilded and velvet-covered chairs, each avoiding the other's glance for a moment as they ordered their thoughts. The square room was not large, but of double height, and overlooked by windows from the chambers of the upper storey. Anyone observing from there—had there been such a person at this moment—might have been struck by the men's resemblance to a pair of brown bears pacing about in a cage.

At length, the Maharaja stopped still, muttering, 'I presume you see this invitation in the same light as I do?' The question was addressed to one of the closed and intricately fretted doorways, but having uttered it, he turned to solicit an answer from his prime minister.

'I presume so too,' Chatterjee replied. 'It is a payment for all those uneaten dinners.' He looked for the quiver of the Maharaja's eyebrows. They were greyer now than when Chatterjee had first learnt to read them, over twenty years before, but still a reliable guide to the royal mood. This seemingly trivial matter of an unwanted invitation, if handled badly, could contain the greatest threat to the Maharaja's personal authority that he had yet faced, and Chatterjee was relieved to see in the twitch of the royal eyebrows that the Maharaja perceived this ... and was amused.

'I think,' Chatterjee resumed, 'the British would say that you are "hoist by your own petard". It's an ugly expression and I've never known precisely what a "petard" is. But you have used your religion against them, and now they seek to use it against you. For what purpose, is not plain. Perhaps they just like to win.'

'So do I, Panditji, so do I. But it's not clear in this game what exactly we stand to win or lose.' He sank slowly into the nearest chair, at a random point in the ring, and twisting sideways in it gazed thoughtfully towards the larger seat that he had earlier vacated. 'Or even what the rules are,' he continued. 'But one thing at least is for sure. We must announce the invitation to the full durbar, as we have said we will. But I have no intention of discussing any difficulty with them, or allowing them to decide the matter. You and I must have a settled view of the response we require from them in advance.'

'Forgive me, Sarkar, but another thing is also sure,' Chatterjee began cautiously, while taking up a seat facing the Maharaja in response to his gesture. 'We know what that response must be. I'm sure you feel it too. This invitation must be accepted. There can be no doubt of that.'

As the Maharaja's frown indicated that he was indeed hearing something he had already understood, his prime minister continued, 'Of course there will be all sorts of bother and nuisance along the way—not least the practical inconvenience to yourself, Your Highness, as you will actually have to undertake an arduous journey. But all these problems we will have to take care of somehow. However great they seem, we cannot let them mislead us into thinking we can refuse the invitation.'

'And what of my caste, Panditji? Is that too a nuisance to be taken care of?'

The tone of bitterness worried Chatterjee, and to give himself time, he evaded the point by pleading, 'Sarkar, these things are not so settled in our religion as people generally suppose.'

'It is what the people generally suppose that matters in such a case,' the Maharaja retorted. 'You and I may feel that it was only fear of the unknown that deterred our ancestors from crossing the sea. That, or their complacency about the known. I do not believe for a moment that I would be polluted by the experience. But I'm sure that many of my people would believe it. And it is the first duty of kingship to be as they wish to see me.' Having reached this point he seemed suddenly less agitated, and continued quietly, as if in sorrow, 'It is not a personal matter but a public one. It is not a question of whether I, Amar Singh, am prepared to break this or that taboo . . . not a question of my personal convictions . . .

but of whether the people consent to my actions. I am their instrument.'

'Then the people will have to be persuaded,' Chatterjee replied firmly. 'They must be made to feel that your going to England involves no loss but is only a glory, and one in which they share. We will have to show them that your action breaks no ban, that it is . . . well, not just acceptable . . . that it is desirable, that it even reinforces orthodox norms.'

But having begun in earnest, he ended with a chuckle to acknowledge the all-too obvious rejoinder, and the Maharaja smiled too as he supplied it: 'And precisely how, my virtuous and learned Panditji, are we going to accomplish that?'

'Hmm . . .' Chatterjee ran the fingers of his left hand down the silk lapel of his tunic and shifted on his chair. For a moment he looked lost in thought, before saying in a tone that was almost frivolous, 'You know, even Lord Ram had to cross the sea . . . to rescue his Sita. It's not a bad precedent.' With another wry smile he seemed on the point of dismissing the thought, but then his expression became more focused as he added, 'Of course, the people believe you to be his descendant, Sarkar. They could be encouraged to see a certain . . . symmetry . . . in your following his example.'

'As I recall, Lord Ram built a bridge . . .'

'Yes, he did. But he also had to placate the gods of the oceans, to ensure safe passage for his party. He made

offerings and performed a special ceremony. Samudra
Pujan.' By now Chatterjee was excited and unconsciously
pulled at his moist collar, as he added, 'Yes, surely that is it...
Sarkar, if you were to perform the Samudra Pujan . . .
it would have to be at the point where you embark . . .
in Bombay, I presume . . . then your journey would be
seen in quite a different light.'

'Wait, wait a moment!' The Maharaja raised a hand
of caution. 'It is ingenious, I will grant you that. Perhaps
too ingenious. Do you think such an action would be
understood? Or understood as we would wish?'

'Certainly,' Chatterjee assured him, and he now saw
the notion more wholly in his mind. 'People still talk
of the Ashvamedh Yagya performed by Maharaja Vir
Singh in Mughal times. He was your ancestor too. He
is reckoned to have been a great king, partly because
he performed the rituals reserved for great kings. Of
course, we would need to educate the public about the
Samudra Pujan.'

'Ourselves too, perhaps,' the Maharaja added
modestly. 'Is the form of the ritual recorded?'

'Oh, *that* can be found out, I'm sure. We can take
advice. Or get young Pandit Haridas to do the necessary
research. It's the sort of challenge he would welcome.'

'Yes, I've noticed his passion. He has once or twice
tried to share with me some obscure matter that he has
found in a text, as another man would show off a new
horse.' The Maharaja smiled approvingly. 'Well, set him

to the task, then. And, who knows, if he comes up with something, we might even ask him to perform the ritual in Bombay.'

The recollection brought him back to his present situation on Apollo Bunder just as Pandit Haridas made the expected signal, pointing to the items lying in front of the Maharaja's folded legs. Taking the cue, the attendant sitting closest to him lifted first a large bale of silk. The Maharaja took it smoothly in his own hands and held it briefly in front of his bowed head, before turning sideways to pass it between the plantain fronds and over the edge of the step, letting it slip gently from his hands into the water below.

The watching throng emitted a collective gasp as it fell. 'Sva-hah!' the pandit declared triumphantly on hearing the splash, and immediately began on the next section of verses from his text. The Maharaja surveyed the remaining offerings arranged before him, all destined to the same end. He mentally rehearsed the sequence: three bronze bowls, each filled to the brim, the first with pearls, the others with silver and gold coins. Attending more to the rhythm than to the meaning of the pandit's words, he again awaited the signal.

He let his eyes wander over the water. Near at hand a couple of small loading vessels bumped as they competed for space at the quayside and workmen clambered over them shouting commands. In the shadow of one, a small boy was grappling with the oars of a rowing boat.

Further out, the steamers waited. Or were some of them moving? It was hard to tell at this distance. They seemed to be in their own silent, still world, animated only by the sparkling light, their purpose so urgent to those aboard, he imagined, but so unknown to spectators. Among them must be his own, the S.S. *Poseidon*, where final preparations for his embarkation were underway.

The thought of the ship reminded him of talking over the plans with Chatterjee, two weeks after their first emergency consultation in the Jalsa Ghar. Meeting at the appointed hour in their usual venue in the veranda of the City Palace, Chatterjee had reported the pandit's delight and confidence at his commission. But while both were pleased with the idea and with its progress, they agreed that it would not be enough. They knew that other doubts and queries would be raised about the method of travel. How could the people be assured of the ritual purity of the ship itself? And how could one maintain an appropriate regime of diet and of ablutions on board during a passage expected to take three weeks?

Having made some preliminary investigations through an agent in Bombay, Chatterjee had proposed chartering an entirely new ship. Thomas Cook and Company, he had learnt, were due to take possession of a new passenger steamer in the spring; but they were open to the suggestion that they might delay its entry into general service and allow it to be reserved on its maiden voyage for the exclusive use of the Maharaja and

his party. Even so, its decks, as yet untrodden by any
sailor or tourist, were to be ritually washed with milk;
and its kitchens, though unpolluted by any cooking,
were entirely refitted. To ensure an adequate supply of
Ganga water, for the Maharaja's personal consumption
and ablutions, Chatterjee proposed commissioning a
pair of vast silver urns that would carry sufficient water
for the round trip.

Extravagant as these gestures were, the Maharaja was
concerned that they still had the air of defensive moves.
The silver urns would be conspicuous items even among
his copious baggage, and would persuade anyone that all
possible precautions were being taken. But they would still
be just that: precautions, safeguards against the possibility
of defilement. It would require something else, something
positive, to effect the transformation, to make the journey
. . . what was the phrase Chatterjee had used? . . . not
merely acceptable but reinforcing orthodox norms.

It was the Maharaja's own idea that he would carry
with him—or rather, as he preferred to put it, that he
himself would follow—an image of Madan Mohan. Ever
since the building of Bhanupur, successive maharajas
had insisted that they were merely the ministers of
Madan Mohan, who was the state's real ruler as well as
its tutelary deity. The invitation to London, issued in the
name of the ruler, was surely meant for Madan Mohan
himself, and where the deity led, his servant must follow.
In the procession from the palace out of the city, in the

train down to Bombay, and in the ship itself, an idol of Madan Mohan would occupy the first position, with the Maharaja following dutifully in attendance. The boldness of the conception momentarily took Chatterjee's breath away. Could this really be done, he wondered? But the Maharaja had told him that the idea could not have come to him from any source other than from Madan Mohan himself. The fact that he, a humble devotee, had been inspired by such a thought, was evidence of the deity's own desire. Who could say otherwise? Thus it was that they resolved to inform the durbar of the Maharaja's intention to attend on Madan Mohan on his triumphant journey.

There were one or two other minor matters that needed to be dealt with, before their way was clear. For instance, there was the problem of the Thakur of Kalwara. A few years earlier, the Maharaja had publicly chided this noble for having travelled to Germany, and had briefly excluded him from attendance at court. As a matter of fact, as the Maharaja now reminded Chatterjee, his objection had been only that the Thakur had undertaken such an ostentatious act without first consulting him, but in the context of the Maharaja's known preference for orthodox behaviour it was widely assumed that he believed the Thakur had lost caste. At the time, he had let this misunderstanding pass. But now, there was a risk of the episode being seized on, not least by the Thakur himself, to vent his disgruntlement.

'But I have a solution for Kalwara,' the Maharaja assured his prime minister. 'I've already sent him a summons to be present at the private audience this afternoon. I propose to ask him to accompany me, pointing out that his experience of foreign travel will be of unique value to us. He will see at once the path to his rehabilitation.'

Chatterjee smiled at this unexpected dividend. He had never concealed from the Maharaja his high estimation of the Thakur of Kalwara's abilities and his sadness that they should be lost to the administration.

But the Maharaja ignored this response. 'My one regret,' he pursued, 'regarding the composition of the party, is that I cannot take you, prime minister. I need you here.' This time the Maharaja did look for the nod of assent, to reassure him that his decision was not unexpected, before continuing. 'I have had a message from the Resident in reply to our indication of our acceptance, saying that he himself will not be going. He feels that the Maharaja and the Resident should not both be absent from the state at the same time. What a delightful image that presents of his idea of his own importance! But I can't leave him to meddle with our affairs for six months without someone to keep a check on him. I rely on you to ensure that he achieves nothing to his credit while I am away. I hope this is not a disappointment.'

'On the contrary, Sarkar, it is as I would wish. And I am investigating the means of our remaining in communication while you are in London. But it does raise the question of who you will take in my place as your personal adviser.'

'I have given some thought to that, and with your agreement,'—he glanced across to catch Chatterjee's eye, knowing how jealously he guarded his position—'if you don't consider it an odd notion, I thought I might ask Colonel Talbot to fill that role. His retirement is overdue and his successor is already in place and champing at the bit, so—well, I won't say that he can be spared, but you can cope without him here. But my main thought was to use him as an interpreter . . . in meetings with India Office staff and so on.'

'Do you have need of an interpreter, Sarkar?'

'Perhaps not. But I've always found it useful that the British underestimate my command of their language. It makes them less discreet, and besides, the process of translating allows greater time for thought. But tell me, if I do take Talbot in that role, how do you suppose he will be perceived by his compatriots?'

'Oh, the Colonel Sahib is highly regarded in official quarters, I have no doubt of that. His length of service alone is likely to intimidate most department officials. I also happen to know that he is due to be knighted—one of a number of awards to coincide with the coronation, I understand. That will only enhance his prestige. Please don't mention this to him, though; he doesn't know it himself as yet. I have it on the authority of Roshan Lal, who works as a bearer in the Residency and keeps me informed of events there.' Chatterjee paused and added with a self-indulgent smile, 'Roshan Lal, like you, Sarkar, understands more English than he pretends.'

'Indeed? A useful fellow, then. But how did the Resident come to be so indiscreet as to mention it within his hearing?'

'Through irritation, I gather. Crabbe and Talbot do not see eye to eye. Crabbe resents Talbot's long presence here and is no doubt on the receiving end of a lot of unlooked-for advice. When he got the communication from London he apparently exploded in front of his private secretary.'

Standing at the stern, leaning over the wooden railing, he liked to watch the wake. Such churning of the ocean had brought the world into being. He had never before understood the image. But then he had never seen an ocean before, much less this strange turmoil of blue crystal and white foam, forever unravelling at his feet, unfolding itself like a map exposed to the searching light of a clear sky. Kingdoms of froth melted at sight, and by the time they travelled to the middle distance, could no longer be distinguished.

The limitless sky awed him. He had never seen it unimpeded, always obscured by buildings. The sky that hung over the courts of his palace was composed of

patches, stretched from wall to wall like shamianas. Even
in the fields of the country—and he rarely visited them
now—the farms and villages were his primary objects,
and the sky was not seen but considered, as a source of
scanty rain. In mid-ocean no human concern divided it.
Only the solitary seabirds hung themselves upon it, and
he marvelled that they could determine their direction
of flight in a world without bearings, a void between
two planes.

It had not been so flat throughout the journey. They
endured a rough passage across the Arabian Sea, when
water and sky merged in a single vortex, his companions
grew sick and suffered more from alarm at the strange
sensation than from the pain of the illness, and he
wondered aloud whether their ancestors were right to
have resisted the crossing of the seas. But after Suez and
Port Said they found the waters of the Mediterranean
calmer, and it felt like passing into a personal eternity.

Of course he knew it to be landlocked—the courteous
Captain Melbourne having shown him their route on
a map—and at times they were close enough for him to
glimpse the coastal cities, first of north Africa, then of
Malta and Sicily. It was strange to think of lives lived
out in unvisited places, of experience invested with
importance but unknown to others. He liked to imagine
citizens, looking out to sea in a moment of leisure,
observing the passing of his ship and idly asking 'Who?
Where? And Why?'

In truth, he had begun to ask these questions of himself, without the benefit of a distant perspective. The enforced leisure of the voyage, and the anonymity thrust upon him by the empty sky, seemed to divest him of all identity. A king without his kingdom. How much was his role as Maharaja composed of what others did and said around him, and the spaces that he filled? Was it only that he wore this robe, in this hall, on such and such a day? Can one still be Maharaja of Bhanupur somewhere off the coast of Malta? Well, no matter. But can one still be Amar Singh? He doubted even that. Beneath the bright and lofty canvas, he knew himself to be only a soul in creation, and perishable as foam.

It intrigued him that some people attributed his rise to fortune—if that is what it was—to some sort of divine intervention or to the fulfilment of a prophecy. Sycophants at court were occasionally heard loudly proclaiming how fortunate the state was that providence had selected Amar Singh to rule over them. Others spoke of the prescience of his predecessor, Maharaja Ratan Singh, who foretold his future role—as if it were something already ordained, when, in fact, it was the result of Ratan Singh's own decision. It struck him as slightly illogical. The idea seemed to be that it was typically brilliant of Ratan Singh to have known something predetermined, while at the same time typically gracious of him to bring it about. He wasn't sure in this case whether the flattery was directed at Ratan Singh or at himself.

In his own mind the sequence of events that led to his adoption involved neither destiny nor prophecy but was almost entirely random. There was even—and he shrank from recalling it—an element of shame. He had never been close to his natural father, the Thakur of Didwana. He did not blame his father for that, gruff and unlovable though he may have been. He knew he was not his father's favourite because he under-performed in things his father valued. He had been sent to the school that Maharaja Ratan Singh had set up for Rajput boys, where the teachers were so exasperated by his lack of progress that they begged his father to take him away. From then on he felt himself to be a disappointment. And he knew that once anyone has been characterized as such there is no way out; it becomes an allotted role. Anything one tries to do will simply aggravate the matter.

Even so, when his father died, his mother insisted that he should inherit his father's title and estates. There was no justification for her to do that. She was not his father's first wife, and he was not even the eldest son, never mind the most favoured. His elder brother had a more legitimate claim in every way. But his mother was from a well-connected family and she wanted to prove her power and influence, to assert herself at last against the interests of her husband's first wife. She was not a woman who would shy away from a quarrel. So she wrote to two or three prominent nobles that she was related to, urging them to support her cause. And against their own better judgement, they agreed to do so.

That was what brought Ratan Singh into the affair. The nobles insisted that the Maharaja himself must settle the dispute between the warring dowagers of Didwana. He might have done so without stirring from his desk. The case was so straightforward—its conclusion foregone—that it required him only to pen a memorandum insisting that the normal procedures of primogeniture be adhered to. But out of deference to the nobles and kindness to the women, he agreed to travel down to Didwana in person and to meet the two boys.

Amar Singh—or Prahlad Singh as he was then called—remembered well the awkwardness of that interview. He had only recently returned from an *akhada* in Vrindavan where he had spent eighteen months in vigorous physical training. He had gone there in the first place largely to get away from home, to avoid being an irritating presence under his father's gaze, and perhaps to spend some time engaged in something that his father might give him some credit for. Whether he succeeded in this last point was something he would never know. It was news of his father's illness that made him return home, and after that he had had only one or two short and unsatisfactory conversations with his father on his sickbed. Or deathbed as it turned out.

He had loved the routine in the akhada. The strenuous exercises presented a challenge that could be wholly absorbing, the focus of all one's mental as well as physical powers. His guru had taught him how everything depended on self-discipline, how, to meet and overcome each set task, one had to be fully prepared in mind and body, and maintain full concentration throughout till the action was complete. He had made him read, not just manuals on wrestling techniques, but more esoteric texts on yoga, and had taught him to see how the mental and physical worlds connect, that in their purest forms thought and action were one and the same. A pure action was a thought embodied; a pure thought an intention to act.

A more visible result of his time in the akhada was his increase in muscle and bulk. He was already taller than his father and brother. This in itself was a source of embarrassment to him: it seemed to mark him out as a misfit, as though he had been cast from the wrong mould. Especially now, watching his frail father dying, he felt his own health and weight to be somehow monstrous.

The comparison with the Maharaja was even more marked. His father had always spoken of Ratan Singh with the utmost veneration, calling him a wise and splendid ruler. Expecting therefore a very regal figure, that day of the Maharaja's visit to Didwana, the young Prahlad Singh was astonished by the bird-like man who appeared. Ratan Singh was so delicate, there didn't

appear to be any limbs inside his clothes. He spoke
softly and tried to be reassuring, but Prahlad Singh felt
he might easily have sat this man on his knee. He was
grateful though for the Maharaja's kind and consoling
manner. He had told him that if he was devout then
God would no doubt assign him his proper role in life,
and that it might turn out to be even more demanding
than being Thakur of Didwana. This was the comment
that people later reported as a prophecy.

Looking back, Amar Singh could not think of it in
those terms. It seemed to him that his mother's ambition
and frankly bad behaviour had brought him to the notice
of Ratan Singh, who remembered him—and remembered
his lack of a role in life—when a few years later, he had to
adopt a successor. Amar Singh did not imagine that any
personal qualities had marked him out for that selection.
What was there about himself that could have appealed
to Ratan Singh, a man so different in every way? The
matter was never explained to him. He was merely told
that he was the duly appointed heir and that as soon
as Ratan Singh died he would become Maharaja in his
place. And he had prepared himself for that task, as
his guru had taught him, in body and mind, and had
remained focused on it ever since. The question whether
he deserved it, or whether he performed the role well, did
not arise in his mind. It was a task that he had been set,
and that he must continue with until it was complete.

'I've decided not to go to Scotland.'

The Maharaja stood at the window, watching the glancing rain freckle the pane, blur the greens of the garden lying below, and deepen the greys of a distant high brick gable. These sights were new to him, though he supposed them ordinary to the permanent residents of this quiet quarter of London. Like the catch and the strings of the sash, they were familiar details in a routine that could last a lifetime, in which he would share for a month or two. The thought of lives one might have lived made him shrug his shoulders. Seen from behind, his bulk filled the frame, the silhouette of his thick flannel jama impressively solid.

'A wise decision, Your Highness, if I may say so.'

'Ha! But *why* do you say so?' The Maharaja now turned to face Talbot, gesturing towards one of the embroidered and gilded little sofas while seating himself in the other. 'Is it such a terrible place?'

'Not at all. I don't mean it as a judgement on Scotland, as you well know, but of our situation. The King's illness is unfortunate, but thankfully not serious. Appendicitis may sound alarming, but I'm assured that the operation will resolve the problem as suddenly as it came on. Postponing the coronation can't be avoided but the delay will not be more than a fortnight. To use the interval for touring might be taken as a sign that—well—that we lack focus on our purpose in being here. We are here to attend on the King Emperor, after all. I imagine that this was Your Highness's own reasoning.'

'Precisely, Colonel Sahib. I have heard that some other Indian ruling princes who are present in London for the occasion have taken leave to travel. His Highness Gwalior, and Porbandar, and a few others, I'm told, are planning to visit the Highlands.'

'Perhaps they could hire a charabanc,' Talbot interjected wryly.

'Well, indeed, it's not a jaunt that it would be dignified to join. But I'm not happy just to sit idle, either. Is there not some assistance we can offer? What is His Majesty's condition? Is he receiving adequate care?'

'He has the constant attention of his personal physician, Sir Hubert Fearer . . .'

'Who is no doubt most assiduous and well qualified,' the Maharaja anticipated the testimonial. 'At least according to your English ideas of medicine. I would wager that he knows nothing of ayurveda. Am I right? Why don't we send our young shastri, Haridas, over to the palace to advise them on matters of diet? He's made a detailed study of such things, you know.'

'A most generous offer, Your Highness, which I will certainly pass on through the Secretary of State,' Talbot replied judiciously. 'I'm sure it will be seen as most thoughtful.'

'But not taken up, eh?'

Talbot spread two plump palms and smiled. 'I'm more concerned to seize the opportunity to arrange a meeting between yourself and the Secretary of State.

With his diary unexpectedly empty and some of the other
ruling princes out of the way, as you say, it should not be
too difficult.'

'Do you have something in mind, Colonel Sahib? Is
there some special matter that you feel I could use the
occasion to bring up?'

'No, not really,' Talbot resumed slowly. 'I suspect that
on such occasions it is better to have nothing—or at least
to appear to have nothing—to "bring up", as you put it.
A man who goes to a meeting with nothing to ask wins
more confidence than . . .'

'Than a man who goes bleating about his neighbours
and about imagined wrongs,' the Maharaja supplied as
his adviser hesitated. 'But you need not worry on that
score. I'm well aware that the Secretary of State for India
has little time for the Empire's loyal servants. Too busy
with the disloyal ones. Your feeling is, I gather, that my
merely appearing before him in the guise of loyal and
suitably reticent servant would be of some benefit.' His
eyebrows raised the question mark.

'Quite so, Your Highness,' Talbot agreed, but his
downward glance revealed him to be embarrassed to
hear their shared assessment stated so bluntly. He
rolled a finger across his moustache and pointed at the
briefcase leaning against the leg of the sofa. 'I've drafted
a short report on public works and reforms undertaken
in Bhanupur in the course of your reign. There's also a
section on the famine relief work that absorbed so much

of our time and resources all last year. If you approve
it—and I've brought a copy to leave with you—then I can
forward it to the Secretary of State's office, so that . . .
you have something to talk about when you meet.'

The Maharaja nodded his appreciation but made no
move as yet to take the document, having some other
matters to address first. 'And what news of the meeting
with the King?'

'Ah! I'm informed that as soon as His Majesty is back
on his feet after the surgery, the proposed audience
with the ruling princes will be rescheduled. There's no
question at this stage of it being cancelled. As a matter of
fact,' Talbot continued while exchanging the brisk tone
for a more cautious one, 'in view of Your Highness's
personal gift for the Queen, there is a thought that you
should be received at a special audience by both Their
Majesties together . . . Needless to say, it is a thought
which I am doing what I can to encourage.'

The mention of his gift brought before the Maharaja's
mind an image of the gold cup and saucer decorated
with coloured enamel that he had commissioned for
the purpose from one of Bhanupur's leading jewellers.
Brilliant ruby-red and turquoise-blue flowers filled a
sage-green and ivory background. A ceremonial sword
with a similar gold and enamel hilt had also been made
to present to the King. Typical of the work for which
Bhanupur had become famous, these gifts had been
suggested by Chatterjee. He pointed out that when the

new King Emperor had visited Bhanupur in person,
many years before, when he was still Prince of Wales,
in the time of Maharaja Ratan Singh, he had laid the
foundation stone of the museum. This gave him a personal
connection with Bhanupur's arts. What could be more
fitting as a gift . . . and more resonant of the recipient's
long association with Bhanupur? Chatterjee also had firm
opinions about which of the city's craftsmen should be
awarded the commissions—particularly on the matter of
the sword blade, to the Maharaja's slight surprise—but
the durbar applauded his proposal. Now it seemed to be
working out even better than had been hoped.

'Are you suggesting that I might be permitted to
present the Bhanupur gifts in person, and in private?'

'My sense is,' Talbot answered in his rehearsed
diplomatic tone, 'assuming the King's swift recovery,
that the idea is now all but approved.'

'Then I must thank you for your efforts, Colonel
Sahib. Chatterjee told me, you know, that your services
would be worth the passage.' The Maharaja stood and
took a slow turn around the room before returning to
his earlier position by the window. So he would get to
meet the King one-to-one. Politically, he knew, it was
insignificant. It was almost a precondition of any such
meeting that it should have no political consequence.
But, symbolically, it was a coup. The people of Bhanupur
would expect no less than that he, as their king, when
going to London, should meet the British king. And

the British too, the ordinary British people—like the loquacious gardener who tended the overgrown acre surrounding this rented house—men and women who knew nothing of the intricate protocols of the India Office, surely they saw him as a king, come from abroad; and for what other purpose could that be but to hold talks with their own monarch? The fulfilment of people's expectations of your role: that was the first but sometimes the hardest duty of a ruler.

The development brightened the prospect of his eventual homecoming, which could now be a triumph. It would now seem in retrospect as though his purpose in going had all along been about more than attending a ceremony. And if the larger purpose was previously not stated, well that is because people of discernment take such things on trust. It would have been unseemly to brag about it.

The thought of his going home led him to a detail which he had so far neglected. People would ask him what he had brought with him—if not by way of diplomatic advantage, at least in terms of material goods. No one came to Bhanupur and left empty-handed. What could the markets of London provide as both evidence and memento of his voyage? Still facing the rain-spattered window, he resumed the conversation.

'Colonel Sahib, I need to do some shopping.'

'What sort of shopping, Your Highness?'

'I was hoping you could advise me on that. Works of art, I suppose. Precious objects. A clock, perhaps. Something to take home.'

'Would you like me to arrange to have some things brought here for you to see? I'm sure I could persuade one of the Bond Street jewellers to send . . .'

'No, I should prefer to go out myself,' the Maharaja cut him off, 'if you feel I could do that safely. I would like to visit some typical London shops. I'm told that Harrods is not far from here.'

'Not far at all.' Talbot gestured vaguely towards the window and then began to sketch a map in the air. 'This road, Campden Hill, leads directly into Kensington High Street which then connects up with Knightsbridge. Harrods is just round the corner from there, on the Brompton Road. But closer by here—just behind us—is Kensington Church Street which might be better for antique furniture or paintings. All told, you are well situated for going shopping, if that is what Your Highness would like to do.'

The Maharaja ignored the hint of disapproval. Some maharajas, he knew, made themselves ridiculous through their prodigal shopping. But in his own case the impulse was not cupidity.

'All the more reason to thank you, for finding such convenient accommodation. Tell me, how did you select it—not for the shopping, obviously?'

'What? Murray Lodge? The India Office had a list of suitable properties available on short lets. I chose this house because it was the closest to Kensington Palace. I hope it is comfortable?'

'Perfectly. Thank you. I especially enjoy the garden—when it isn't raining. Mr Dilkes—the gardener, you know—has been giving me lessons on British plants. Birds, too. He proudly showed off his raspberry canes and pointed out a pair of magpies—his chief opposition in tending them. Rather like our mahalat except that it's black and white.'

'Yes, I'm familiar with magpies. And I'm glad they are a pair. We have a saying about them: one for sorrow, two for joy. So, a good augury for your stay here, Your Highness.'

It was raining again two days later as Talbot struggled up the flight of steps by the side of the Red Lion near Lancaster Gate, juggling to keep the umbrella over both his head and the large portfolio that was slipping from his arm. He paused under the awning of the Taormina restaurant to secure his grip and allow the squall to subside. He had forgotten how insidious English rain could be, creeping coldly under your collar, providing none of the sense of grateful relief that you got from a monsoon shower in Bhanupur. Once the force had reduced to a drizzle, he set out resolutely on the last stretch into Queen's Gardens, and soon stood under the stout columned porch of the Royal Asiatic Society, ringing the bell and shaking his umbrella.

Inside, he found Constable already installed in the librarian's front office, seated behind the large oak table that was spread with volumes he had taken down from the handsome bookcase labelled—with a small ivory plaque—'Tod Collection'.

'It's amazing what you can find here!' Constable declared by way of welcome, as though continuing a conversation begun earlier, though in fact he had not seen his friend and colleague since his own retirement and departure from Bhanupur over three years before. 'Just look at this. It's an autograph letter of Vir Singh II. Priceless!'

Talbot took the proffered page in one hand while laying the other lightly on his friend's wrist to acknowledge the unspoken greeting. He glanced at the sloping lines of writing without really trying to take in their meaning and for just long enough to allow both men to adjust to their reunion.

'I've got something to show you, too, which I am sure you will find just as exciting. If you can make a little space on the table . . .'

Constable obediently gathered up the bound manuscripts and collected them in a pile as Talbot put his portfolio in their place and untied its ribbons. One by one, he extracted a series of large sheets of paper, each covered with geometric and floral designs painted in brilliant hues. Deep crimsons, peacock blues and chrome yellows seemed charged with Indian sunlight in the gloomy London room. Once the surface of the table was covered, Talbot began to lay the pages one over the other, creating a cascade of flowers in vases, of meandering scrolls of strap-work, of arabesques and grotesques.

'Your carpets,' Talbot announced proudly, if redundantly, since his proposal to get draughtsmen to paint details of the carpets found by Constable had been the subject of much correspondence between them. The photographs that he had commissioned earlier, though wonderfully rich and glossy as images in themselves, conveyed nothing of the colours of the carpets and were judged quite inadequate for the kind of publication that Constable had in mind. So Talbot had next suggested engaging pupils from the school of art to paint them in gouache. But if the drawings were expected—indeed impatiently awaited—the degree of fidelity to the originals was something Constable had not reckoned on. Rather than attempting to depict a whole carpet on a single sheet, the artists had selected individual motifs and reproduced them at full scale, and in doing so seemed to give equal attention to every individual knot and thread.

'You can see the pile quite clearly!' Constable declared in astonishment, adding as he gingerly laid a finger over a surface, 'It's hard to believe you can't feel it, too!'

'I fear they may lose just a little of their impact in being printed,' Talbot warned. 'Of course if we use chromo-lithography the deterioration will not be marked.' Though pleased by Constable's enthusiasm he felt the need to restrain it. The printing would be expensive and he already foresaw that they would have a battle in persuading any publisher not to cut costs by reducing the size of the plates. 'We should take them to Briggs, don't you agree? They did a fine job with your jewellery book and they are still the leading publishers of this kind of thing.'

Constable's eyes were so close to one of the leaves that he had to tilt his head to reply. 'I don't know of any other printer who could even begin to match this quality of colour. They are so sumptuous!' He stood back as if to take in the whole tabletop of images at once, and Talbot saw his friend's face register a sort of ecstasy.

Later, when they had carefully gathered the sheets together and packed them safely in the portfolio, they spoke of other news and plans while browsing through the librarian's shelves, taking down volumes at random. Talbot did not feel quite adequate to the task demanded of him to 'report all the gossip from the court', or of saying whether 'that old rascal Chatterjee was still up to all his usual tricks'. Feeling obliged to produce something more than a dismissive gesture, he conceded that there was increasing anxiety in Bhanupur over the lack of an heir to the throne. Twenty years into his reign,

the Maharaja had many achievements to his credit,
particularly in promoting education and the arts, but he
had still not provided the essential successor.

'Of course you knew about the Maharaja's College
getting a license to issue BA degrees, because that
happened before you left—in fact your museum collection
was a factor in making it happen. But now they've started
admitting Master's students as well. It's practically a
full-fledged university in its own right. People appreciate
this change. It means they don't have to send their sons
away to Calcutta to get them educated as they can get
an equivalent degree at home. And even those whose
children don't have what it takes to benefit still feel proud
at the College's reputation. But there are rumblings
about the lack of a Yuvraj.'

'But it's not as though he's already too old to produce
children, surely?' Constable remarked, doing a quick
mental calculation.

'Heavens, no! He produces children in quantities
that would satisfy anyone. Just that none of them are
legitimate. The mother's always a concubine, not a
recognized maharani. Your friend Chatterjee is very
discreet but I suspect he's not at all pleased with the
situation. Every time a new baby is born he tries to hush
it up and it's a rash man who offers congratulations
on the happy news. Meanwhile, he's under constant
pressure from the Resident to bring up the matter of
succession with the Maharaja—which he is loath to

do directly. There—that's some gossip for you,' Talbot added, conscious that he had gone a little further than he intended.

Far from making him feel in the swim of events, this report brought home to Constable how much he missed his days in Bhanupur, how his life since his departure had felt like a permanent exile.

'And what about yourself, Talbot?' he asked, a little despondently. 'Are you going to hang on a while longer yet?'

'Actually, no. It's not official yet so you may not have heard. Having travelled here with the Maharaja, I shall return to Bhanupur with him, but only to clear my desk. I've been appointed by the imperial government to conduct a survey of irrigation networks across the whole of Rajputana. Apparently someone in the India Office feels that after thirty-five years in Bhanupur I need a change of scene. Or that Bhanupur needs a change from me.'

'It will be a great loss to Bhanupur.'

'Not really, though it's kind of you to say so, Constable. The deputy engineer has effectively already taken over my role. Chap called Stoker. He'll be confirmed in office as soon as we get back.'

'I'm sure he won't be half so active as you have been all these years.'

'He has his own skills. It's true he doesn't seem very interested in keeping the architecture office going and he's planning to lay off some of the draughtsmen. But in fact you know the architecture side has already been largely taken over by our old friend Banwari Lal.' He paused for a moment, deciding not to elaborate on that aspect of the matter. 'Roads,' he continued. 'That's Stoker's great thing. Wants to build pukka roads all over the state, serving every little district town. A bit like you with your dispensaries.'

'Well it's certainly worthwhile—and not unconnected from dispensaries. It would help a lot with delivering medicine if people could get around more easily. So I wish him luck. But tell me more about your irrigation survey.'

'It seems the young Maharaja of Bikaner is pushing the idea of a major new canal system through the northern part of the desert. The plan has implications beyond his own borders, so I've been deputed to gauge its impact, assess any likely benefits to the region as a whole. But nothing's been announced yet so please keep it under your hat for the time being, eh?'

Constable smiled his assurance, but then all abruptly looked agitated.

'I say, my dear fellow . . .' he almost stuttered. 'Speaking of things being announced—many congratulations! I should have said so at once. I saw the coronation honours list just a couple of days ago. Probably the best deserved knighthood in the empire!'

Talbot laughed, relieved that his friend's pleasure was so obviously no pretence. Even so, he offered the self-deprecating explanation he had prepared. 'It's meant as compensation, I think. For dragging an old man out of his study and putting him back in the saddle under the sun. But it makes me happy for Stephanie, of course. *Lady* Talbot and all that.'

'Has the Maharaja said anything about it?'

'Yes, as a matter of fact, he has. Offered me his congratulations most warmly as soon as the list was published. He has this way though . . . he somehow managed to imply that he had known about it for quite a while . . .'

Constable looked a bit blank, but then said with a chuckle, 'Perhaps Chatterjee has a spy in the India Office. I wouldn't put it past him. Or else in the Residency,' he added, suddenly looking more serious. 'There's a fellow who works as a bearer there, I've once or twice caught paying more attention than he ought. Pretends he doesn't understand English.'

'I think I know the man you mean. In fact I mentioned it to the Resident once but he wasn't interested. Rather implied I was interfering. You noticed, I suppose, that the Maharaja's got one too. Not a spy, I mean . . . a knighthood.'

'Yes, I did indeed. Star of India, no less.'

'Quite right, too. A knighthood fit for a prince! Mine's a KCIE of course: also available to office-wallahs.'

Inside the walled city, the bangle-sellers of Lal Chowk were agitated. Even on normal days the clustering of their shops in the square's north-western corner was a mixed blessing. With some of their wares displayed on poles suspended in the shared veranda that ran along the front of their cell-like stores, they created together a glittering show that enticed more customers to their row. But the customers were fickle and, to the dismay of the seller whose stock they had first approached, were easily distracted by the colour and shine of his immediate neighbour's. But such tensions were far from the bangle-sellers' minds today as the swollen crowd that surged in the square lapped against their thresholds, and jostling elbows threatened to upset the delicately balanced poles and the carefully piled boxes filled with tinted glass and lacquer. With any sharper jolt the shopkeepers could not help crying out, but anxious not to cause offence and miss a sale they tried to make their protests sound more like warnings.

'Arrey, madam, please take care or you will cut yourself. This is all the finest glass!' . . . 'Madam, please sit inside and be comfortable. There is so much crowd here.'

To make matters worse, they knew perfectly well that the shoppers today were not serious. Fingering the sparkling bangles was just part of the entertainment of the day out, a distraction that would be abandoned as soon as the main show—the procession—began. It was tempting to shut up shop and join the throng. But none of the traders actually did this . . . partly, perhaps, out of some residual hope of making that unlikely sale, but more from a resigned sense that staying open and being part of the side-show was their allotted task for the great day.

Closer to the centre of the square, people pressed up against the fencing recently erected around the perimeter of the old step-well. A group of youths tried to jump up and grasp the top of the boards in their fingers to haul themselves up. One or two had succeeded and were perched uncomfortably on top, gesticulating extravagantly as they yelled advice to their companions below.

No one had used the well for years. The once-familiar sight of women carrying pitchers and descending the stone steps that lined its inner walls was now but a memory, as the new handpump that stood nearby and the many others located at street corners throughout the city had rendered the arduous task unnecessary. Putting up the fencing had marked the well's official closure, but there was still some doubt as to what would happen to it. Some people said that the prime minister had plans to fill it in and have a garden laid out over the top. Others complained that this would spoil the character of the square, and that the whole idea was typical of Chatterjee, an outsider who didn't understand the traditions of the city at all.

A policeman waving his lathi was trying to get the attention of one of the boys sitting on the fencing, shouting to him to climb down. But his tone of command did not carry conviction; indeed, he was visibly desperate. The task of trying to marshal the crowd was overwhelming. There were people everywhere. At one point the road was jammed by an ox-drawn purdah cart. With no driver in sight, the policeman did not know who to approach to demand its removal. Presumably the female occupants were still inside—perhaps they had even given instructions to be parked and left here, expecting to watch the procession from their private vehicle—but he could not think to part the curtains and investigate. He consoled himself with the thought that no one would blame him, and they were not directly obstructing the procession's intended route. Anyway, he knew from experience that once the procession appeared the crowd would miraculously part to make way for it.

The procession was due to enter the square from Jai Pol Bazaar. The leading band would give notice of its approach. Next would come the Maharaja on his elephant, surrounded by the cavalry guard, with the household guard on foot bringing up the rear. If the way was clear they might attempt a full circuit of the square, which would delight those who—hours in advance—had already taken up position in the windows and balconies of the buildings on its further, eastern side. Failing that, they would only have to manage the section in front of the bangle-sellers, as they would leave the square from the north, down the gentle slope of Sadar Bazaar, past the Jhanki Mahal, to the entrance gate of the palace beyond.

Spotting a number of his colleagues already stationed by the bangle-sellers, the policeman decided he had better

stay where he was. And then a half-heard conversation
reminded him of the additional duty he had been
charged with besides traffic management. Just behind
him a red-cheeked tradesman, sweating under his stitched
pagri and delicately holding up one corner of his brilliant
white dhoti, was telling his companion, with much
emphasis, that today was a red-letter day for the city, that
the Maharaja's voyage to England had been a great thing
for Bhanupur, but having him back again was even better.
His companion—a thinner man in spectacles—looked
unconvinced and muttered something about 'a nice
chance for a tamasha'.

To the policeman's ears the cynicism sounded
a little forced. He recalled that he was supposed to
report all such comments to his superior officer, to
help the government gauge the public mood, but he
felt that he could fairly suppress the tamasha jibe as
untypical. Most of the people seemed happy enough,
didn't they? In truth, he wasn't fully sure. Maybe he
was just reflecting his own loyalties. But he could not
help sensing that the crowd, frustrating as it was to try
and control, was animated by good humour as much as
impatience; and that everyone—even the busy chickpea-
sellers—seemed charged up, in anticipation not just of a
spectacle but of something that was in some mysterious
way to their advantage.

Ranged in orderly rows along the carriage drive, the
flower pots of Khasa Kothi gleamed like sentries. Close
inspection would have revealed many of the plants to be
wilting, as with intermittent monsoon showers they were
alternately waterlogged and scorched. Finding it hard
to anticipate and adjust, the mali focused his efforts on
painting the pots so that they shone when wet, drawing
the eye away from the limp greenery and creating the
impression of a cheery welcome.

The Maharaja had sent advance word of his intention
to pause at Khasa Kothi—placed as it was between the
railway station and the walled city—to allow himself
time to rest after the journey, but also to give adequate
notice to the citizens of his planned triumphant re-
entry through the streets to the City Palace. Chatterjee
had responded to the news with more obedience than
enthusiasm, ordering a rapid cosmetic renovation of
the main hall and the front garden. The work was
overseen by Banwari Lal, though not without some
mild protest on his part, judging it less important than
other commissions that he had in hand. Chatterjee
had managed to persuade him by implying that he fully
agreed that the architect and the task were unsuited to
one another, but what could he do, the Maharaja had
specifically requested Banwari Lal's services. And in the
end the prime minister was able to say with conviction
that the new layout of the drive, with an approach from
the northern side, did seem to lend the building a more

imposing aspect, and gave it something that had always been lacking.

The Maharaja evidently felt it too, remarking almost as soon as he alighted from his open carriage that the place was looking better than it had for years—though the mali might benefit from some advice on the selection of seasonally appropriate plants. Chatterjee knew that he had been over-optimistic in hoping that this last detail might escape attention in all the clamour of arrival. His own head was still pounding with the noise of the crowd and he wondered at the Maharaja's composure. For the railway station, hung with bunting, had been thronged on Chatterjee's orders with groups of schoolchildren waving banners and shouting 'Long live the Maharaja!' in carefully coordinated choruses. All along the road they had been cheered by marshalled rows of citizens who took up the refrain as the carriage passed, until the shout seemed to meet its own echo like the phrases of a round-song.

Even as they sat in the freshly painted hall, on sofas draped in starched white cotton, they could make out the distant shouts of people excitedly awaiting the procession. Chatterjee mentally reviewed some of the final preparations that he had set in motion before leaving for the station. The elephant, already painted and caparisoned but still tethered by the ankle in the stable yard, was being photographed by the man from Rajputana Studios. Man and beast were equally unnerved by the

unusual encounter, and neither felt encouraged by the
hoots of hilarity coming from the group of youths who
had managed to climb on to the yard wall. Meanwhile, the
silver howdah, shining like a mirror, was being needlessly
polished again by two men who applied themselves to the
task with the energy of wrestlers. They were watched and
subjected to a mocking commentary—'Missed a bit!'. . .
'Who's getting married?'—from members of the cavalry
guard, who had been prepared for hours but were trying
to keep up a mood of eager anticipation.

If Chatterjee himself felt uneasy it was nothing to do
with the planning of the procession—he was confident
he had done everything necessary—but because he had in
mind the report he had despatched to await the arrival
of the Maharaja's ship in Bombay, and he knew there
was one item in it that the Maharaja would want to
raise, here and now, before making the final stage of his
journey. Chatterjee could not in good conscience have
left the topic out of his account of events in Bhanupur
during the Maharaja's absence, especially since he had
been expressly charged to monitor the activities of the
Resident. And even if it made for a sour welcome, in
truth he had found it easier to address the matter in
writing, having so often in the past avoided bringing it
up in face-to-face discussions.

'So, Panditji, it seems that Mr Crabbe has been
bothering you about the succession again!' the Maharaja
began with what sounded to Chatterjee to be a slightly

forced cheerfulness. 'I must say I think that is unhelpful of him, especially when I am away from the state. How does the man expect me to produce an heir when I am away from home? Unless of course he fancies the idea of a half-breed Yuvraj . . .'

Having acknowledged the introduction of the expected subject with the smallest nod, Chatterjee shrank from the indelicacy of the last remark, but then rallied to the task he had set himself.

'As I tried to intimate in my report, Sarkar, the Resident unfortunately chooses to link the question of the succession with . . . other matters. While you were away, one of Your Highness's consorts—one residing in Vijaygarh—was delivered of a son. I did what I could to keep this news out of general circulation—and at least it was successfully kept out of the press—but somehow it came to the ears of Mr Crabbe. And he makes of it what he chooses. He seems to regard the keeping of concubines as an obstacle to the birth of an heir. He states quite bluntly that Your Highness should attend more to the Maharanis . . .'

'Does he indeed? Does the man think he is running a stud farm? I'm not a horse, you know, Chatterjee.'

'Yes . . . yes . . . I quite see the impertinence of his comments, believe me, Sarkar. What worries me is his tendency to imply that damage is done to your personal reputation by . . . by the Vijaygarh factor . . . and that any such damage outweighs the good you have achieved by making the journey to London. Suppose he were to express this attitude in an official report . . . it could do us material harm.'

'Oh, I doubt it, you know, prime minister. I honestly doubt it. My sense is that the India Office is far less concerned about details of my personal life than Mr Crabbe is. Not just him—Residents past and present. The Residents get obsessed about Vijaygarh, but I don't believe that London shares their interest.'

Chatterjee was struck by the conviction of this speech. Here was a new confidence, a man secure in his position, sure of being better informed than those around him. If the Maharaja implied that he knew the mind of the India Office better than its distant officials, this was not unreasonable in the circumstances, with his having been so recently and closely in touch. But Chatterjee already sensed there was more to it than this, something that would not wear off with time.

'And I will tell you something else,' the Maharaja continued in a lighter tone. 'Mr Crabbe is not only more obsessed with Vijaygarh than London is. He is more obsessed with it than I am myself. He has much to say about what he calls libidinous activities—I know it, you don't have to spare me the details. But to be perfectly frank with you, that kind of passion has never been central to my life. This may surprise you. It would certainly surprise Mr Crabbe to know the truth. He thinks I'm debauched. I wouldn't be surprised if he's telling London that he's convinced I am going to die of syphilis. But, you know, I'm happy to let him weave his scurrilous fantasies, and I don't mind who believes them. People reveal the tenor of their own minds by what they believe. My conscience is clear.'

Chatterjee was silenced for a moment. He sensed that the Maharaja's smile and his levity were merely the last two remaining veils held before a personal revelation, and he wished to avoid any embarrassment. 'It's not a matter of realities,' he began tentatively. 'Perceptions also matter, Sarkar . . .'

'I'm sorry to hear you say so,' the Maharaja broke in. 'It seems to me that only realities matter in the end. And the reality is that I simply do not understand—at least I do not share—a view of the world that places private passion first. This view seems particularly prevalent among the British, which may be why they are so quick to attribute it to everyone else. Quite honestly, it means nothing to me.'

As he ran his thumb smoothly along the underside of the broad satin sash bound across his chest, he seemed to Chatterjee to be momentarily absent-minded, distracted by a memory, and when he spoke again he confirmed the impression.

'While I was in London, Colonel Talbot took me one evening to see a stage production. It was a play. *Romeo and Juliet*. I expect you have heard of it, since you have read so many English books. Talbot told me that it was

one of their great classics. Well, I had to concede that
the poetry sounds very fine. But the story struck me as
absurd. Two people die for love. What is the use in being
a dead lover, if you have never been anything else? What
is achieved by making passion so central to your being
that you are defined by it? When I asked Talbot what
Romeo's profession was he said I had missed the point.
Well, perhaps I had. But it seems to me we are ultimately
defined by the work we do. I have always felt defined by
the role that was handed to me when I was adopted, and
I live that role every moment—whatever the Mr Crabbes
of this world may choose to believe.'

'I can attest to that,' his prime minister assured him.
'But if we are dealing with realities then I don't think we
can dismiss so lightly the views of Mr Crabbe.'

'Why do you hide behind Mr Crabbe?' the Maharaja
broke out. 'Why don't you tell me your own views? I know
you have wanted to raise the matter of the succession
with me for years. I've seen it in your eyes.'

The forthright tone briefly stunned Chatterjee. 'Well,
Sarkar,' he began cautiously, 'if I may express a personal
view . . .'

'That is precisely what I have just asked for.'

Refusing to be thrown off-stride, Chatterjee launched
himself, almost with relief, into a speech he had so often
rehearsed. 'It is my fervent hope and prayer that you
will be blessed with an heir. And soon. I would hope
to see the child grow up, the path of his development

settled before . . . well, before either of us leaves for the heavenly abode.'

'The heavenly *what*?' The Maharaja sounded contemptuous. 'Why is it that whenever you Bengalis speak about death you sound like Christians? Obviously in Calcutta you live too close to the British. I have no aspiration for a heavenly abode. I consider samsara to be a central article of our religion. My own fervent hope and prayer'—he echoed the phrase deliberately, without satire—'is that having performed my duty in this life, I may be born in the next as a poor Brahmin and work as a humble servant in the temple of Madan Mohan. The temple which I have the honour to serve in this life as its patron. I should like to sweep its floor.'

As Chatterjee was silent he resumed, 'Have I shocked you?' But then, recollecting the main point at issue, he added, 'Ah, no. I see I have digressed. I haven't answered you. Well then let me set it out clearly so that you need not be in doubt any more. I decided a long time ago—and on this voyage I confirmed in my own mind—that when the time comes I will adopt. As I myself was adopted. Adoption saves time. I could adopt a boy ten years old, even twenty. And it is consistent with our customs. I refuse to father an heir because that would give too much authority to the mother within the zenana and too much influence to her male relatives outside it.'

Having declared this much resolutely, he added more ruefully, 'All this nonsense about Vijaygarh . . . Of course

I admit that the place affords me some comfort, but it is really meant as a distraction for others. It is a convenient device to explain the absence of an heir to minds like Mr Crabbe's.'

'Are you telling me,' Chatterjee asked in astonishment, 'that you deliberately cultivate his misunderstanding?'

'I regard his misunderstanding as unimportant. What is so terrible about being misunderstood? Is life only about what others think of us?'

'What would you say is more important?' Chatterjee was now agitated. 'Surely you are not going to say what a man thinks of himself?'

'It depends *where* he is doing the thinking. Standing before a mirror—no. We are apt to judge ourselves leniently. But what a man thinks—or knows—about himself when standing before his God . . . or his king, perhaps . . . at any rate, a more severe judge than himself . . . Well, you should know, you have been a schoolmaster. You are accustomed to making boys feel shame.'

Chatterjee briefly felt this last comment as a barb, but quickly recognized it as a deflection, a signal that the conversation was closed. He glanced at the Maharaja inquiringly, waiting for the new direction. When it came, the tone was positive.

'Since we are back to the subject of perceptions, you and I, Panditji, have a public perception to create this very day. I'd like you to ride in the howdah with me. The king and his minister will parade before the people and enter the city. Come, it's time for me to go home!'

❀

From an awkward position, with his head hanging in the empty channel, and with one foot, one knee and the palms of his hands planted on the ground by its rim, Talbot looked up from under his arm to announce to the bulking figure of Chatterjee, 'It seems fundamentally sound. A few cracks in the plaster here and there but they look superficial. You could probably get away with patching rather than resurfacing the whole thing. There's certainly no need to relay the brickwork behind.'

Discomfited by his own comparative comfort, Chatterjee leaned over his companion slightly in a token gesture of participation. Grateful as he was for Talbot's professional advice he silently wished that he did not enter into these tasks with such zeal. He was always so confoundedly fit and energetic and it made Chatterjee feel sedentary. He much preferred meetings indoors.

Talbot pushed himself upright and balanced on his haunches while he rubbed the dust from his hands.

'Of course, the only real way to test any water system is to run it,' he continued. 'That way, you see at once where the leaks and seepage are.' Standing up, he gave a slight tug at the tails of his tunic. 'Are we sure about the source of the water?'

In reply, Chatterjee simply stared blankly, as if the question was not one for his portfolio. Why was an expert hydrologist asking a prime minister about water?

'It's not entirely clear, you see.' Talbot began to explain. 'There's an old well-head in the corner of the garden over there'—Chatterjee pretended to look in the direction indicated but made little effort to discern the object pointed out—'but so far as I can make out there's not enough space there to have bullocks turning a Persian wheel. It's too close to the garden wall. So it might have been used as a secondary source but it can't have been the main supply for the channel. There's a large tank on the roof of the main pavilion and that seems more likely but I can't work out how it was filled. It would have been very laborious to fill it manually, bucket by bucket. Hard to imagine that being the intention. So there must have been a pipe . . . and of course a source that it was attached to.'

At last Chatterjee remembered a piece of information that might be pertinent. Diffidently he offered it:

'I'm told that there is a natural spring somewhere on this hillside. It's part of the same system that feeds the bathing tanks at Ghitorni. Could that be what we are looking for?'

They both looked up and scanned the rock face that loomed disconcertingly close and dark. The garden had been built on a narrow terrace at the foot of the hill, part of the range that fringed the city on its eastern side, guarding the main road to Karauli. One side of the garden overlooked the road. On the other, the hill rose abruptly, its northern face permanently in silhouette. While the intention, no doubt, had been to place the garden so as to give it a sheltering back wall, the natural feature dwarfed the artificial and seemed to threaten it with imminent destruction.

As it turned out, time rather than falling rock had proved to be the enemy. Built at the same time as the city for Bhanupur's first prime minister, Brahma Dutta, the garden had long been abandoned and allowed to decay. No descendants had laid claim to it and its ownership had reverted to the state—or was assumed to have done so—but for a century and a half no one at court had thought to restore it or make any further use of it. Until now.

Chatterjee's plan was to open it to the public. He had especially in mind foreign visitors, whose favourable impressions he considered important to the state's prestige. Bhanupur was famous for its elegant gardens but tourists were often dismayed to find the largest and most important one—the Vir Niwas behind the palace— teeming with local people who went there to worship at the temple of Madan Mohan. Privately, Chatterjee's sympathies lay with the devotees but he still felt it his duty to accommodate the prejudices of visitors. Restoring Brahma Dutta's garden would give them a sanctuary to enjoy in peace and quiet, away from the thronging multitudes. The slightly sombre nature of the place he actually found quite appealing; and anyway it would be softened with running water and gushing fountains. He liked as well the associations of the place—that it was once the property of another prime minister, and another Bengali at that—but these thoughts he did not voice. He did not need to: it was already whispered in parts of the city that 'Chatterjee obviously fancies himself as a second Brahma Dutta. He's going to spend his time lounging in a garden drinking sherbet and watching dancing girls.'

Chatterjee dabbed at the nape of his neck with a handkerchief and shook it in the direction of the shade of the small pavilion on the garden's farther side. 'Shall we?' he invited his companion.

The two men walked shoulder to shoulder at a stately pace as much to avoid the scattered debris as to give a pause to their activity. Disturbed by their approach, a cattle egret inspecting the lawn quickened its step and then launched itself into the air, gliding a few feet above the ground and alighting to resume its search in a distant corner. Entering the pavilion, Talbot rubbed a thumb against a coloured plaster dado and grunted his approval—whether at the design or at its preservation he did not say. The men settled themselves in the folding chairs that had been placed in the pavilion for the purpose—hardly the scene of luxury that Chatterjee's detractors had in mind, but welcome enough for the present.

'Really I am most grateful to you, Colonel Sahib, for your help . . . as always . . . I wonder how we will manage here in Bhanupur when you are gone!'

'With no trouble at all,' Talbot replied jovially, 'It's me who will be missing *you*, prime minister. Bhanupur has been my home for almost all my working life and it will feel very strange working anywhere else.'

'But you've had a foretaste of that,' Chatterjee pointed out, seizing on the lead. 'I mean with the coronation visit. I've been meaning to ask you, by and by, for your impressions of all that.'

'Ah!' Talbot thought, 'so this explains why our learned babu invites me out into the sunshine which he is known to detest. Not just so that I can advise him about a cracked drain but so he can pick my brains about the London visit, away from prying eyes and eavesdroppers. I might have guessed.' To give himself a little time he raised and joined his hands, as if in prayer, fingertips to his lips, and purred.

'I will, if I may,' he began—glancing across at Chatterjee—'answer your larger question at once by declaring that His Highness acquitted himself remarkably well throughout the tour.'

Chatterjee's embarrassment at the bluntness of this comment was more than offset by his relief at the verdict and by the understanding it established that they could speak freely. For the moment he sought only one clarification.

'What do you mean by remarkably?'

'Well . . .' Talbot could not help but laugh at his own imprecision, but chose to justify it: 'His Highness's demeanour throughout was in fact the subject of much remark, not least by Their Majesties themselves. I think they really warmed to him. He's not the sort of maharaja . . . I mean, speaking frankly between ourselves . . .'— Chatterjee offered an open hand as encouragement to proceed on that basis—'he's not the sort of maharaja who gets on readily with British nobility . . . or even officials. This is surely no secret. But he deported himself with great dignity throughout and earned respect as a result.'

But Talbot was not satisfied with his report and soon resumed. 'It's more than respect. You see, it's easy enough for the King to get along with Indian princes he can talk to about shooting and hunting. You remember His Majesty was here himself in his youth—well, we were all much younger then—back in '76 when he was still Prince of Wales. So he's got a fund of pig-sticking and shikar tales to draw on. And he's happy with a maharaja that he can share those things with. Or just someone whose command of English puts everyone at their ease. Our man is not like that. But in a strange sort of way the King really liked him for being different. For being himself. And the Queen simply adored him. He made no attempt at phoney gallantry. He was rigidly polite. And she thought he was magnificent. 'Every inch a king!' was her assessment. That caused a flutter in Whitehall, I can

tell you. We're not supposed to recognize maharajas as
kings or even as royal—in our parlance they are Princes
and Highnesses—so the comment won't be placed on the
record. But she clearly meant it.'

Satisfied by this picture of cordial relations, Chatterjee
still felt a material point had been ignored.

'But you gave Their Majesties, I hope, a copy of the
report that you had written on all the work we have
done—that the Maharaja Sahib has sanctioned—in
matters of irrigation and famine relief . . . the roads and
railways we've built in recent years . . .'

'Of course I did, prime minister, and I've no doubt
they will read it. But you know'—again the joined chubby
hands went to the lips—'please don't imagine . . . don't
misconstrue this, but such things matter much less to
Their Majesties than they do to us. Even the India Office
just notes and files such reports. Every maharaja the
length and breadth of India has someone like me writing
reports that portray their state as progressive and soundly
governed. Some of them are even true—including ours,
of course. But if the India Office receives them all with
the same indifference, we shouldn't take it amiss. We
do the work, after all, not for them but for the people,
who benefit directly. Its political value . . . well, I know
we talk about that but to be honest it's pretty negligible
by the time the news reaches London.'

Chatterjee's gaze dropped to the marble floor, but
he raised it to survey, through the pavilion's arches,

the darkening hillside. It's true, he thought, any noise made here must be pretty faint by the time it reaches London. At this moment, the very idea that the places were connected seemed preposterous. But despite that, he knew the connection was a fact, and one that he had to deal with. He roused himself for his last question:

'Since you mention the India Office . . . did anyone there raise the matter of the succession?'

'Yes and no,' Talbot began cautiously. 'No, in the sense that I've listened to the Resident's concerns since I got back—about children born in Vijaygarh and all that—and I have to tell you that the India Office regards all that as so much irrelevance. Crabbe does himself no favours by drawing attention to such things, especially in the light of the Maharaja's reception in London, at the palace . . . but Crabbe won't take advice from me. But, yes, the India Office is concerned about the succession. Not in any melodramatic way. Their assumption is, at this point, that when the time comes, His Highness will adopt a suitable Rajput boy . . . just as he was adopted himself. That should be fairly straightforward, shouldn't it?'

1922

1922

'The situation has changed somewhat, Panditji.'

Chatterjee considered this remark a gross understatement in view of their immediate surroundings, even if that was not what the Maharaja had in mind. Far from the graceful comfort of their usual meeting place in the City Palace, they now sat under dripping canvas with mosquitoes buzzing in their ears. The humid air hung heavily about them and Chatterjee was miserably conscious of the state of his clothes, moist with sweat and spattered with mud. He had travelled down the very bad road to Ratangarh for only the second time in his life, in great discomfort; and not even his sense of urgency could stop him resenting it.

'What change—if I may ask, Sarkar—justifies your spending an entire month in the middle of the monsoon living in a tent? And in a place so remote from everyone who has a just call on your attention?'

Chatterjee paused. Though convinced that reason was on his side, his querulous voice sounded in his own ears like that of a man aggrieved, and he had no wish to depart from the long-ingrained habit of deference. He swallowed a rising gorge of sarcasm.

'I'm sorry that my actions disappoint you, Panditji,' the Maharaja replied, showing no matching restraint. 'I might point out that I am here on pilgrimage. It is not supposed to be luxurious, you know. If I had wanted comfort I have palaces to go to. It is not unusual for pilgrimage to be a little arduous.' He pulled a large silk handkerchief from the sleeve of his jama, as if to mop his brow, but used it instead to add flourish to his gesture, pointing through the tent wall as he continued. 'As for my being away from the centre of things . . . I am here to visit the temple of Peepli Mata, whose divine intervention—you may recall, Panditji, since you've studied our history—helped Bhuvan Rai to found the kingdom. Far from being remote, this valley is the very epicentre of our state. Though I will concede,' he added with a chuckle and a marked glance at Chatterjee's clothing, 'it's a little hard to get to.'

The shrine of the goddess, built into the side of the hill, had been where Chatterjee went first on his arrival. Indeed he knew well the legend of how she had aided Bhuvan Rai in his battle against the Meenas, by bringing back to life those of his soldiers who had been killed by the Meenas' arrows. The story was recited to every

schoolboy in the Maharaja's College. More interesting
to Chatterjee, was the temple itself, consecrated to her
in thanksgiving. One of the oldest buildings in the state,
it had stood for a thousand years and had long outlasted
the removal of the capital and of the ruler, first to Jamner
and later to Bhanupur. It was a place that encouraged
historical reflections and long perspectives, and the
primeval face of the goddess seemed to hint at even
further aeons, unknown to the human mind.

Standing at the top of the steps outside the shrine,
after making his brief obeisance, Chatterjee took in the
view of the Maharaja's encampment, which brought his
thoughts back to more immediate matters. The steep
and wooded little hills—pinkish and brittle-looking in the
gaps between the verdure—gave some shelter to the camp,
straggling across the narrow valley. The high flat screens
arranged in a rough circle towards one end indicated
the makeshift zenana, the headquarters of Nargis. The
Maharaja's current favourite and delight—it was said—the
former dancing girl was a source of nothing but vexation
to the prime minister. Many at court believed her to be the
author of the plan to visit Ratangarh in August. Chatterjee
was unsure about that, but felt that the rumour itself was
damaging enough, and so was the pilgrimage. In any case,
Nargis was nothing more or less than a public enemy, and
he noted her position on the field of contest.

At the other end of the camp stood the Maharaja's
own tent, an elaborate but hastily patched-up affair, made

with a mixture of service khaki canvas and fine brocade panels. On the top perched a little cloth turret, from which fluttered the multi-coloured pennant, the signal of the Maharaja being in residence. A vast and ancient kadamb tree rising behind provided shade from the open southern end of the valley.

Whatever little enchantment nature gave the scene from a distance quickly dissipated as Chatterjee approached. The ground was waterlogged. As he squelched towards the royal tent, Chatterjee had to keep pausing, to try and chart out a way ahead, only to find it barred by another trough, forcing either a retreat or a desperate leap, and neither of these reactions added to his dignity or prevented him from getting still filthier. Conditions were greatly aggravated by the large number of animals roaming freely around the tents. The camels, having carried all the camp's paraphernalia from the city, and with nothing further to do until the time of return, had been let loose and ambled about nonchalantly. Sheep and goats, brought for the kitchens, waded through the mud in search of something to graze on, their last meal before the slaughter.

Even as he fretted about the state of his trousers, Chatterjee had realized that the threat to the Maharaja's well-being was even greater than he had estimated. Camping in the rain was one thing. But unsanitary conditions like this had been known to defeat armies of fit young warriors, never mind, let's face it, a sick old man. His Highness's health was a cause of concern at the best of times, despite the adoption. True, the formal recognition of a Yuvraj meant that the Maharaja's sudden demise would no longer precipitate a crisis; but even so, the prince was no more than a boy, after all, and the Maharaja's illnesses were still alarming. On entering the tent and being received, he had tried to make his inquiry sound routine—he hoped that he found His Highness well, etcetera—but this had merely prompted the ambiguous response about the situation having changed. Watching him now, wiping his glistening face with his handkerchief, and grimacing—as though exhausted by the effort involved—Chatterjee began to fear that he had come too late.

'Sarkar, you do not look well. Please . . . I beg you to consider returning to the city where you can get some proper medical attention.'

'I am perfectly well attended, thank you. Haridas Shastri is here and visits me every hour. He gives me repulsive herbal infusions to drink . . .'

'May I ask the Residency surgeon to come? I'm sure if I explain . . .'

'Certainly not. I have no need of English medicine. Never have had, and least of all now.' Seeing Chatterjee about to persist, he continued, 'And what would you explain, precisely? What can you know of my real condition from your own observation? I'd thank you to insist no further, Panditji. Besides . . . I assume that there is some pressing matter of business that has brought you all this way through the rain, to disturb my devotions. You had better tell me what it is.'

The sharp tone was belied by the smile that accompanied this demand. It still amused the Maharaja to corner his prime minister, to push him to the point he was not ready to address. And though discomfited by being made to seem so transparent, Chatterjee too was pleased to find the Maharaja's combative humour intact.

'Your Highness, the council . . . and the nobles . . . are naturally concerned by your long absence . . . and by the risk involved, to yourself . . .'

'If that is a further reference to my state of health,' the Maharaja broke in, 'I have already asked you not to concern yourself. What else troubles the court?'

'There is a perception, Sarkar . . . and as I say it is only a perception . . .'

'Yes, yes. Of what?'

'That the idea of the pilgrimage was not entirely your own. Some of the nobles are openly objecting that you have allowed your partiality towards a certain member of the zenana to mislead you . . . allowing *her* to mislead you, perhaps I should say. There is a suspicion that she has ulterior motives in bringing you here.'

'Of course she has,' the Maharaja replied promptly. 'She hopes I'll die.'

Chatterjee's sense of relief at having found a circumlocution to express his fear was shattered by this terse announcement. His embarrassment—for he knew that putting it all on the nobles was unconvincing and a shade dishonest—was replaced in an instant by utter astonishment. The Maharaja looked gratified by this response, and resumed in an almost jocular tone.

'She has looted—or so I am informed by the Keeper of the Wardrobe—a fair number of state jewels, and she keeps them with her in a box. She has brought me here, in these foul conditions—and, yes, I suppose I must agree with you about all that—in the hope that if I die here she will be able to get away in the confusion, taking the jewels with her. If we were in the palace, she would have no chance of escape.'

Chatterjee stared at him in bewilderment.

'You look puzzled, prime minister,' the Maharaja continued in a still more animated voice, obviously enjoying himself. 'It's really quite simple. She won't entrust the jewels to any accomplice; she must keep them with her. But she would have no means of getting either them or herself safely out of the palace once I'm dead. Hence the pilgrimage. Slipping away from here . . .'

'Yes, yes, I understand how the plot works, Sarkar. As you say, it's simple enough. What I don't understand is why you are allowing it to proceed. If her motive is what you say, why did you agree to come to Ratangarh?'

'Because I have a motive of my own!' The Maharaja's defiant declaration was accompanied by a flick of the wrist and a conjuror's shake of the handkerchief. But he immediately softened, and added more sombrely, 'A motive which, perhaps, I owe it to you to explain.'

Chatterjee's expression had not changed. The Maharaja's animation, at first reassuring, was beginning to alarm him. He could barely articulate the request, 'Please do.'

Now that he came to the point, the Maharaja hardly knew how to tell him. The starting point for him had been the Lalwani petition, but their dealings with that still left such a sour taste—for Chatterjee as much as for himself—that he did not wish to remind him of it. The substance of it was bad enough on its own. That it should have come from such a source . . . from Gopal Narayan Lalwani, a respected trader, a member of a group of citizens he had always sought to promote, in whom he placed his greatest confidence . . . made it all the more painful. Had he not cared for their welfare? Had he not always sought their approval and guidance? And then to have Lalwani quote scripture at him! . . . 'If the King does not care for the traders they become lost to him, and leaving the kingdom retire into the woods.' Frankly he doubted whether Lalwani would last very long in the woods. Much too accustomed to the comforts of the city. But it was only rhetoric anyway, these references to the Mahabharata. The demands in his petition showed clearly enough that

he had abandoned any real sense of tradition, and that
was what really hurt.

He remembered an earlier, happier time, when they
had agreed on such matters. He had spoken to him
shortly after his return from London, when Lalwani
had attended a morning private audience to take his
blessings, having just been appointed as private tutor to
the Thakur of Nimbaj. The Maharaja had advised him
to keep a balance in what he taught the young noble,
between traditional learning and modern knowledge,
and not let one dominate at the expense of the other.
And Lalwani had smiled and said, 'Sarkar Sahib, keeping
the scales level is just what we traders do!'

He had liked the analogy but thought even then
that it was not only traders who knew the importance
of balance. Selecting the appropriate mode for each of
his actions, being at one time progressive, at another
conservative, was the very tenor of his rule. When,
just recently, he had sanctioned the extension of the
railway line from Danta to Sajjangarh, a few were heard
to grumble about 'durbar interference', but most were
pleased and said how it showed that this Maharaja had
a vision for the future. And they were the same people
who had marvelled at the Gangaji shrine that he built
next to the Madan Mohan temple, saying that it was
built in the proper old style, that it looked as though it
could have been built by one of his great ancestors in the
time of the Mughals, and that they were glad they had a

ruler who kept to traditional forms and did not try and change things just for the sake of change.

But Lalwani had lost his sense of balance, his respect for the old ways. His impertinent petition showed he had mislaid his precious scales. No doubt he could quote Sanskrit shlokas in every second paragraph, and no doubt that fooled some naïve readers, but it was really nothing more than a list of demands for change. The very fact that he published the wretched document, that he was not content to write privately to the prime minister—which was his right to do, if he had genuine problems, even his duty, some would say—but he tried to get around the durbar and appeal directly to the people . . . well, that showed complete disregard for all established norms.

The absurd thing was that many of his demands were not unreasonable, and were already being addressed. So he wanted more telegraph and post offices to be opened in the city. And he wanted more pukka roads and railway lines in the state. All of that was being provided. The Maharaja conceded—at least privately—that it was harder to make headway in such matters since Talbot had left. His replacement, Stoker, was competent enough, but there was something unsatisfactory about the man. His attitude to work was all wrong. He seemed to regard his post as a job rather than as a life. For Talbot everything was a mission and the Maharaja missed his enthusiasm. But his replacement by Stoker didn't mean that the work had stopped, and any reasonable person would agree that Lalwani's grievances were exaggerated.

What really showed Lalwani's lack of balance, though, was his criticism of the School of Art. He had contemptuously dismissed their fine products as 'curios for extravagant travellers', or some such phrase. Did he not realize that the arts were the engine of the city's economy? That they made people like Lalwani rich? He could think of several of Lalwani's close associates who were in the gem trade, and who had prospered in it. Where would they be without the School of Art to showcase Bhanupur's arts to the world? And when he—the Maharaja—had commissioned that jewelled sword and cup to present to the British King and Queen, what was he doing but promoting a trade that supported the people of Lalwani's community? To call them *curios!*

Worse still, was his effrontery in criticizing expenditure on the zenana, implying that maintaining a zenana at all was improper in this day and age. It is all very well for the trading classes to have their own standards and household traditions, but to seek to impose their limited morality on their rulers is obscene. As for his complaint about the locking of the city gates at night, suggesting that the custom made Bhanupur look ridiculous in the eyes of progressive people like the British . . . well, he was surely wrong about that. It is just the sort of tradition the British approved of. They may not want it in their own cities—they don't even have gates anymore, come

to that—but it is the kind of thing they find charming
and appropriate in a traditional place like Bhanupur.
The criticism stung, though, implying as it did that the
Maharaja was unaware of British perceptions, when he
had always been so adept at gauging them.

One thing, for sure, that would not have impressed the
British was that slogan Lalwani raised about 'Bhanupur
for Bhanupur's own'. He wanted all senior posts in the
administration to be reserved for men born in the state.
Such provincialism! Bhanupur had always developed
on the strength of imported expertise. Why should it
change that policy now? Lalwani himself, ironically, was
of immigrant stock, which made his position absurd.
No doubt the man himself had been born in Bhanupur,
but how many generations of his ancestors could he
count as 'Bhanupur's own'? His family was living
proof of the value of the city's tradition of welcome to
foreigners. But Lalwani clearly wasn't thinking about
men of his own community. Though it was disguised by
a complaint against the people who ran the state railways,
the real target of his attack was clearly Chatterjee. A
nasty, insidious little barb. The prime minister himself
had bravely muttered something about having broad
shoulders, but beneath that cloak of indifference he had
taken it sorely.

And there was more. Page after page of what Lalwani
called 'just demands' that were 'long overdue'. Some of
them were transparently demands for further opportunities

for the merchant classes to enrich themselves. He wanted a
state bank to be set up, and a mining industry established.
Actually, those ideas were not bad in themselves and
might be worth looking into one day, but the Maharaja
was damned if he'd be pushed into such undertakings
by the likes of Gopal Narayan Lalwani.

And then, buried amid a whole lot of verbiage about
regulating exchange rates and oversight of the police
force, there was that demand—the most outrageous of
all of them—to have a Legislative Assembly. Lalwani
seriously and solemnly proposed making the state
administration a matter of debate, of public discussion,
among 'representatives' elected by the citizens! He had
not cared to explain precisely how he thought that a
bunch of elected nobodies would be able to administer
more effectively than a carefully selected, hand-picked
group of experts such as the state already had. Indeed, it
would be difficult to imagine how they would be able to
conduct any work at all: it would be non-stop argument
and division. Lalwani obviously hadn't seen that. He
merely insinuated that what he called the people's
participation in government was some sort of right. That
it was 'overdue'. And then he had the effrontery to insist
that he was not a revolutionary. He claimed to be loyal
to the 'beloved ruler' and not in the least bit inspired
or instigated by the 'drastic changes' now occurring in
parts of British India. But it was as plain as the ink on
the page that the nationalists were the real force behind

this, that they had fed Lalwani with ideas. They were bent on pulling Bhanupur down with the Raj, and men like Lalwani were merely their chosen instruments.

But no, that's not really it . . . Even in his rage, the Maharaja knew that assessment to be unfair. Lalwani was no fool, nobody's puppet. No doubt he was in touch with nationalists from outside the state, and perhaps he even took some encouragement from them. But if he espoused similar causes it was because he really believed in them. And he was not alone. Men like Lalwani were not trouble-makers . . . at least they did not set out to make trouble for its own sake. They remained what they had always been, what their ancestors were: honest brokers. They were traders who knew the value of fair dealing. But their views were changing, their aspirations, their ideas about how they wanted to be governed, were all in flux. And in this they were part of a wider pattern. One could not insulate Bhanupur from changes taking place across the whole of India.

Should one even try? Much as he detested the very idea of Lalwani's talking shop, and preferred to trust his own judgement in finding the right man for each task, and much as he enjoyed laughing with Chatterjee, as together they mocked the rhetoric and the naked self-interest of Lalwani's 'just demands', still the Maharaja recognized that this cheeky pamphlet reflected a far greater force than itself. Something had to give, and the thought wearied him.

Even as he marshalled his arguments against the touted reforms, the Maharaja began to question whether he was still in tune with the times. He worried that his cherished balance was no longer the instrument required. Times had changed. The citizens had changed. Even the British had changed. The oafish new Resident, Reginald Slater, could barely conceal his delight at Lalwani's petition. He pretended to be outraged, of course, and muttered something about dark forces, but it was obvious to the Maharaja and to Chatterjee that he agreed with its main thrust. He seemed to claim no stake in Bhanupur's traditions, as if he were indifferent about their very survival. Such men would be quite useless as allies in confronting change.

But after all, was confrontation necessary? Perhaps change could be managed in some way. But not by me, the Maharaja confessed privately, his gift for self-knowledge leading him to his most depressing conclusion. Some new approach was needed to face the future, one that he did not possess. Was he himself the object that must move? After all this time, was *he* now the obstacle to be overcome?

And that had been his new starting point. He need not go over all this again with Chatterjee today, not least because Chatterjee loathed Lalwani personally and was still smarting about that Bhanupur-for-Bhanupur's-own business. It would only make him angry. And so Nargis was a useful diversion. She was vexing in a quite different

way. He would continue for a while with her, to lead him
to the point.

'I should first let you know, prime minister, touching this
matter of the jewels, that I have no intention of gratifying
the lady. At least not as far as the theft is concerned.
There is no room for doubt about it, by the way. She is a
thief. And I'm sure that as a responsible minister of state
you will be pleased to hear that I will not protect her from
the consequences of her own actions. No doubt, in time,
the law will take its own course and exact its price. I may
not live to see it but I can ensure that it happens.'

'May not live?'

'May not live . . . No doubt when she is apprehended
she will find some consolation in my having fulfilled at
least part of her plan. For, difficult as it is to explain . . .
and hard though it will be for you to grasp, for all your
mental powers . . . well, the plain fact is that I did come
here to die. Not actually *here* in Ratangarh, of course . . .
in the palace. I'd prefer to die in my bed. Coming here
was just a necessary part of the process. Haridas assures
me that I already show every sign of having contracted
pneumonia. As soon as I am convinced that he has given
up any hope of my recovery I shall order our return
to Bhanupur.'

The last phrase was spoken matter-of-factly, as if it
concerned any routine journey. But neither this nor the

puckered eyes misled Chatterjee into thinking that the Maharaja was trifling with him, that it was all in jest. He had not mistaken either the pain or the determination in that phrase, 'I did come here to die'. But seeing the fact did not help him see the reason. He felt more lost than ever and it was as much as he could do to whisper pleadingly, 'Why, Sarkar?'

Gesturing to Chatterjee to stay as he was, the Maharaja rose from his chair to pace about on the carpet laid over coir matting. The handkerchief hung limply from the hands now clasped behind his back.

'It's a fair question, Panditji, and I shall answer it, not only in recognition of the work you have done for me over many years but to prepare you for your role in what lies ahead. And yet, despite our history I have to ask you again to set aside, for a moment, any personal feelings you may have. I have thought about this matter logically and I hope that you will too.'

Chatterjee responded to the interrogative tone with a slight nod. With all his heart he wanted to cry 'No!' But he needed to know what this supposed logic was all about.

'When I said the situation had changed,' the Maharaja resumed, 'I meant that for some time now . . . ever since the end of what the British call the Great War . . . a rather conceited phrase—don't you think?—as if no one else had ever had a great war . . . well, since the end of the war there has been a marked change in the British.

It seems obvious to me now that they will leave India . . .
perhaps not tomorrow or the next day . . . but soon. They
will give in to the nationalists.'

Again Chatterjee detected a hint of a question,
as though he were being asked to corroborate this
assessment. 'Are you suggesting,' he asked in reply, 'that
despite winning the war in Europe the British are losing
the will to rule?'

'The will? No! Will is a commodity the British always
have in abundance. We may even see it strengthen in the
short term. But that cuts against the underlying grain.
They may assert themselves even more aggressively, but
that will only be because they feel in their hearts that a
decision has already been taken—by some among them
. . . some of their own—that they should leave. And it's a
decision they cannot resist. In truth, I think they see it as
the only honourable course. It fits with everything that
they have to say to *us* about representative rule. Or rather,
their staying looks more and more like a contradiction
. . . looks like a contradiction to *them*, I mean, never
mind how it appears to the nationalists. All we are left
with now is the normal delay between decision and
action. Momentous change is hard to effect . . . people
are accustomed to the way things run. It's always easier
to keep things going on. But the deed catches up with
the thought in the end. And my guess is that moment
is not far off. Twenty years at the outside. Maybe less. If
they get embroiled in another war—with the Russians,

perhaps—then that might slow the process down. But that doesn't look likely at present, and of course it might even speed things up. As you see,' he concluded with a chuckle, 'this is hardly a prophecy. I cannot be precise about the timetable. But it will happen, and within a generation. Of that I feel certain.'

Chatterjee was suddenly aware of having spent time in recent months subconsciously resisting this idea—that the British might eventually leave—even without formulating it as such. He had argued in his own mind against a view which he had not dared articulate. And this recognition alone now persuaded him to admit its truth.

'Yes, I see. The British will leave. Even so, Sarkar, what has this to do with . . .?'

'Ah, I'm coming to that. Have patience, prime minister.' The Maharaja continued to pace in front of his audience. 'The departure of the British raises the question of the Princely States. It's all very well for them to abandon their own provinces. But what about Bhanupur? They have a treaty with us, remember, which they will have to honour. It's not up to the British and the nationalists alone to determine what happens to us. They will have to negotiate with us.'

'Quite so, Sarkar . . . and who better to represent our interests than someone with your long experience . . .'

'No, no,' the Maharaja interrupted him, 'that's just the point. To get the best deal for Bhanupur, we need a ruler who seems appropriate from *their* perspective, not ours. You win the trust of the British by being as they want you to be. My forty years of rule will count against me. I will seem to them like a relic of the past, not the herald of the future. You don't need experience, you need youth.'

'Thank heaven for the Yuvraj, then. But, after all, he's only ten. Rather too youthful . . .'

'Not at all! I chose a boy of ten with a purpose in mind. Listen, Panditji, the conclusion may be hard to accept—believe me, I wish it could be otherwise—but the reasoning is clear. Here is the crux of the matter. The British like a state best after a period of regency rule. A minor on the throne and a council packed with Englishmen actually in charge. Government by committee. The fact that they generally mess it up is beside the point, because they don't see it like that. Now . . . if there were to be a regency council in Bhanupur over the next decade, it would give the British a stake in Bhanupur . . . align them with our interests. Bhanupur would become one of their projects. They would also manage the education of the Yuvraj and think more highly of him as a result. They would consider him their creation, their man. When he comes of age and gets full ruling powers he will be ideally placed to negotiate on behalf of Bhanupur. He will be the right man presenting a case in which the British will already feel they hold a vested interest.'

'I cannot fault your logic, Sarkar,' Chatterjee responded dryly. 'As always, your reasoning is impeccable. There is but one slight flaw, don't you think? It has occurred to you that the man who will initiate this regency council is the current Resident? We've had some hopeless men in that post over the years—I always thought Crabbe was one of the worst—but Reginald Slater!' He hung his head in exaggerated despair.

'He has no imagination, I grant you that. But he will manage the mechanics of it rather well, I think. And his lack of insight is actually an advantage to us. It's important, you see, that he should feel that establishing the council is his initiative, rather than something he has been led to. You have a role to play here. This is what I was alluding to a moment ago. You need to bring forward a few people now . . . men like that Pandit Achal, in your office . . . give them a little more prominence, a bit more responsibility. Not overtly, just so much that Slater notices them. Then, when he selects them for the council he will think he is plucking them from obscurity.'

'Advancing men like Achalji will be both easy and a pleasure . . .'

'But that will be near the limit of your role, my friend. Like me, you are too much a part of the old regime to be part of the new. You will have to excuse yourself from membership of the council and try and keep an eye on it from outside.'

Chatterjee instantly saw the truth of this but felt its abruptness sharply and his dismay showed on his face. 'What need have I for retirement?' he asked almost bitterly. 'What would you advise me to do with my time?'

'Why don't you write a scholarly catalogue of your fine collection of arms and armour?' Mingling warm encouragement with light mockery, the Maharaja's tone revealed that he had not thought of this proposal on the spur of the moment. 'That would take your mind back to the old days and your friendship with the good Dr Constable.'

'I wasn't aware that you knew about my collection.'

'Oh?' The Maharaja laughed. But he did not want to tease Chatterjee for long. 'I heard of it from Haridas,' he confessed. 'You must be aware that he's friendly with . . . what's his name? . . . that man who used to be the clerk at the museum . . . Kashinath.'

'Ah . . . . Kashinath,' Chatterjee repeated softly, still disconcerted. 'But why does this formula not apply in your own case?'

'I don't follow you, Panditji. What formula?'

'If one accepts the force of your argument . . .'

'I thought you had already admitted its logic.'

'But I'm not yet ready to accept its implications. It seems to me that your conclusion must be your own removal from the scene, Sarkar, but . . .'

'Exactly, prime minister. Clearly put! The course of events I describe is obviously desirable, and the only obstacle that stands in the way of their inevitable fulfilment is me. I must therefore, as you say, remove myself.'

'But it does *not* follow that you must wallow in mud until you catch pneumonia and die! This is monstrous . . .' But his rising anger, his outrage against the Maharaja's continuing air of reasonableness and calm, left Chatterjee searching for words.

'What would you propose instead, Panditji? Maharajas don't retire. They can abdicate, of course, but in practice only when there's a scandal. You have to shoot some woman's husband or be grossly incompetent or corrupt to be asked to abdicate. Is that what you would advise? And even if you were to insist that none of these situations apply . . . that I was not abdicating for any of these usual reasons . . . no one would believe you. There would be the taint of scandal come what may, a scandal that would attach not just to my name but to Bhanupur, and so undo half the advantage gained.'

'And does no scandal attach to suicide? Yes, let us call it what it is, Sarkar. You are committing suicide. Is that an honourable course?'

'Ah! I seem to recall we have discussed that question before . . . a long time ago . . .' The Maharaja was a little chastened by Chatterjee's anger, but he was not deflected. 'You can call it what you wish . . . I would prefer to think of it as a sacrifice. In any case, I do not believe that my death will be seen as a case of suicide. It will be seen by most people—especially by the British, whose opinion will drown out everyone else's—as the natural and inevitable outcome of my supposed debauchery. My lifestyle is considered a scandal, too, but a very minor one . . . one that everyone's been used to for a long time.'

The Maharaja smiled and the hint of jocularity returned as he continued, 'You know, Panditji, I'm rather pleased with this aspect of the whole thing. I've been cultivating this misunderstanding of my personal life all through my reign—despite your protests—in case it should turn out to have any use. I now see what that use is to be, and that the long nurturing has been worthwhile. What you once called the Vijaygarh factor explains my passing. It leaves no room for mystery. That's why, incidentally, I seized on the idea when Nargis proposed coming here to Ratangarh. People will say—you tell me they are already saying—that I was too much under her influence. Well, excellent, if that helps them to understand, to accept it . . . Even the lady herself believes that I am her instrument. The fact is, of course, she is mine. I needed her, to give me a plausible motive for staying here . . . so long.'

The last phrase was uttered wearily, and seemed to surprise even its speaker. 'I'll grant you another thing, Chatterjee,' he added. 'This is a ghastly place. I ache to go home.'

As if to emphasize the point, the Maharaja had slumped back into his chair, and planting his elbow on the chair arm, clasped a broad hand across his forehead. Chatterjee watched the hand, rubbing the temples and then drawn down over the cheeks and the almost matted grey beard. The weary eyes that looked up forced him to lower his own.

For a while the two men sat in silence. Even from the camp, no sound could penetrate the hot columns of still air. Chatterjee was twice on the verge of asking where and when they would meet next—vaguely in his mind was the idea that at some future moment the Maharaja might take a different view—but he stopped himself, knowing the question was futile. They would not meet again.

To distract himself from this thought, he busied himself with practical details.

'What would you have me do with the lady, Sarkar?'

'Deliver her . . .' the Maharaja replied at once with a ready answer, 'into the hands of whoever the council appoints as its legal member. Only on a charge of theft, mind you. No other charge.'

'And if she tries to abscond?'

'My guess is that she'll come quietly. She may be gloating on her power now. But her life will not be worth four annas in the streets of Bhanupur after my death . . . and even less inside the zenana. She will see prison as her safest option.'

With this matter settled, Chatterjee relapsed into silence. He rehearsed in his mind the prospect put before him. The Maharaja dies. The Resident sets up a regency council and supervises the education of the Yuvraj. And then when the moment comes for the British to leave India, Bhanupur has a young Maharaja, well liked by the British, and well placed to negotiate the best terms for Bhanupur's future. The plan was so simple. Clear-sighted. But still he broke out in revolt.

'Does it really have to cost your life . . .?' Chatterjee did not recognize his own voice . . . not that of a prime minister, but of a pleader.

'I paid with my life long ago, Panditji. It is spent. I've served the state daily for over forty years . . . as you know well . . . you've served every day of it alongside me . . .' Again it was clear to his listener that the Maharaja had earlier asked himself this question. 'I did not seek this role,' he continued, 'It was thrust upon me . . . But I accepted it as my duty. So to fail to take this last step, this last thing required of me, in the interest of Bhanupur, would go against everything that I am . . . everything that I have become.'

This time Chatterjee did not answer, and his silence seemed to signal assent.

'I won't pretend it is an easy choice, Panditji . . . and your gloomy visage doesn't improve matters,' the Maharaja resumed with a forced cheerfulness. 'But don't you think we tend to exaggerate death?'

Chatterjee's raised eyebrows were enough to prompt
the Maharaja to pursue the thought. 'Our mortality . . .
the very inevitability of death . . . makes us accord it great
significance. But logically it ought to have the opposite
effect. The fact that death comes to each and every one
of us ought to make it seem banal . . . And I suppose it
is the banality that helps us get over it, after a while. Tell
me . . . has any death ever caused you lasting grief?'

'Talbot's,' Chatterjee mumbled promptly.

It was the Maharaja's turn to look briefly surprised
as he commented, 'Talbot . . . he was a good friend to
Bhanupur . . . he is certainly missed.'

But that was not the point at all, Chatterjee thought.
He did not grieve for Talbot himself but for the widow he
left behind . . . for Stephanie . . . who now had no one
to stand between her and the memory of her lost child.
Chatterjee felt her bereavement as a personal loss, and
though he would never speak of it—certainly not now—he
often imagined her alone in the cottage in Evesham . . .
the cottage that Talbot had bought when he returned to
England at the time of the coronation. Talbot had told
him about it so proudly after they got back, saying how
he had prepared for his eventual retirement. Wanting to
show an interest, Chatterjee had asked, 'And this place
Evesham, is it anything like our Bhanupur?' But Talbot
had only grunted and looked disconsolate. So Chatterjee
could not feel sorrow on Talbot's account when the news
came from England that he had died. He was a man who

knew his life's work was complete. Perhaps that is what the Maharaja means . . .

Chatterjee felt himself giving way, the argument overpowering him by some insidious means, like the dampness of his clothes. He looked around the tent as if in search of some support, but its very fabric struck him as an outrage.

'Is this the way, Sarkar?' He knew the question to be his final bid. 'All this squalor . . . this self-abasement . . . is this really the way?'

'The way?' The Maharaja seemed puzzled by the choice of word. 'No . . . it's not the *way* . . . I suppose you're right about that, at least, Panditji.' And then, in a level, almost pedantic tone, he explained, 'My death . . . well, yes, *that* is the way . . . in so far as it is a means to an end . . . But what you call the self-abasement . . . no . . .' He paused momentarily before adding a further thought: 'Of course, I can see that sometimes self-abasement might be a way . . . Sometimes . . . sometimes no doubt it *is* the way . . . But this time it's the destination . . . I was not born to kingship . . . I must end as I began.'

He caught his companion's eye and smiled faintly—a smile that Chatterjee knew well, that he had seen so often over the years, and that showed the Maharaja was once again both pleased and amused at the course their talk had taken.